THEIR HAND IS AT YOUR THROATS

John Shire

Invocations Press

When suddenly in the midst of life comes a word never pronounced before, a dense tide gathers us up in its arms, and there begins the long journey into newly-initiated magic, which rises like a scream in an immense abandoned hangar, where moss clothes the walls, amidst the oxide of forgotten creatures which inhabit a world in ruins.

Alvaro Mutis
A Word.

THEIR HAND
IS AT YOUR THROATS

John Shire

Published by Invocations Press
© 2013 John Shire

978 095680215 6

Design and pictures – John Shire
'Set' in 10 on 12 Bookman Old Style.

Limited Edition of 100 copies of which this is

71

CONTENTS

PREFACE

The Alternate Manuscript · **5**

Investigations · **15**

Beneath the Black Tower · **29**

Among the Pavilions of the Great Khan · **49**

Generation · **63**

The Tip of the Iceberg · **93**

What Danforth Saw (Or 'A Final Plunge') · **111**

Lovecraft, Lacan and the Lurking Fear · **135**

Signs and Signals · **147**

Irrevelations · **165**

After Summer · **187**

AFTERWORD

PREFACE

...STORIES AFTER LOVECRAFT

For almost thirty years I have been trapped in the orbit of a vast dead star named Lovecraft. And it's driving me mad. After any number of futile attempts at mapping its protean geography, I finally decided to put my efforts into breaking away instead. But it looks like that's never going to happen either.

Look, what do you need here? Surely, now you've got past the title, I don't have to explain who Howard Phillips Lovecraft is? Writing is difficult enough, let alone writing about my own writing about someone else's writing. This collection does not have 'Lovecraft' or 'Cthulhu' in the title. Which I see as a good thing. In fact, I do try (though occasionally fail) to avoid those convulsions of speech and spelling that are so easily and regularly adopted. The source of *Their Hand Is At Your Throats* may be obvious but 'Stories After Lovecraft' seems an apt subtitle too, both plain yet faintly cryptic. However, several of the more historical stories in here are deliberately set before the dead star was identified; returning to a time when encounters would make no sense and have no context, as indeed, they never can or should. I enjoy the opportunity of returning to surreal images, made bloodless through high-culture acceptance and over-use, a fittingly psychotic intensity (like Machen's roses that sing theory). But there remains the vast terrain of Lovecraft studies, the myriad reading communities: should I address them? That's what the stories are for. What would Cthulhu do?

While particular encounters will never produce exhaustive explanations, these stories would not exist without some very specific books. Gabriel Ronay's *The Tartar Khan's Englishman*, Peter Fleming's *Bayonets to Lhasa*, Benjamin Woolley's *The Bride of Science,* a biography of Ada Lovelace, and Joscelyn Godwin's *Arktos* have all played roles that will become obvious and are well worth reading in their own right. The two pieces here that could be considered non-fiction may, I suppose, border on the pretentious, the archly postmodern, showing off a winking intertextuality. Well, I think it's fun.

Truthfully though, trapped here in the teeming void that surrounds Lovecraft, I realise that I've always understood him – the Universe at once malign and indifferent, understood yet made terrible through scientific endeavour. All it proves to me is that we only have each other. And therefore that must be enough: a humanist perception.

And there's nothing quite like ending on a positive note.

But don't despair. None of what follows does that.

ACKNOWLEDGEMENTS

The Alternate Manuscript first appeared in *Cthulhu Codex 10* in 1997, *Investigations* in *Darkness Rising: Night's Soft Pains*, 2001, *Beneath the Black Tower* in *Book of Dark Wisdom 6*, 2005, *The Tip of the Iceberg* in *High Seas Cthulhu* (Elder Signs Press 2007), *Signs and Signals* in *Lovecraft's Disciples 6*, 2006 (reprinted in *Cthulhu's Creatures* (JnJ Publications 2007) and *After Summer* in *Cthulhu Codex 15*, 1998. Versions of *Lovecraft, Lacan and the Lurking Fear* have appeared in *Crypt of Cthulhu V16 #3*, 1997 and *V19 #3*, 2000. Everything else has remained unpublished until now.

Endless thanks to all those editors who allowed me in, particularly Robert M. Price, Mick Sims, Joe Pulver and William Jones.

Inevitable thanks to Mike, Vicky, Tanya, Ella, Gideon, Cyril, Rod, Andy, Pete, Mum, Wig and Richard.

THE ALTERNATE MANUSCRIPT

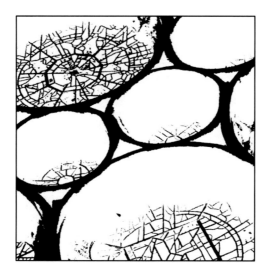

This file is the transcription of an interview conducted with Neville James Paige (subject 32-a-Lon.), a twenty-six year old male currently under Shadow Detention (Criminal Justice Addition Vol. 3 Sec. 15) in the interests of State Security. Current text is restricted to International levels only - fully updated Starlight clearances required. Subject was arrested with three others (Detentions 35-b, 35-c and 38-c(1) – ref 31/3 Lon.) during a Service raid on 75b Castle Street, Dec. 28th 1994 – location restricted to SL5 and above. No judicial hearing required (JA 5, sec. 14). Subject is summarily guilty by admission, circumstance and evidence of five murders, including all aspects of 'New Religious Torture' and proselytization. Interview conducted by Dr. Alan Marshall with text subsequently revised and expanded by subject to qualify as legal statement.

Reference files: Fractal Dynamics/Time (general 57 and 465-8f), Visions (general 46), Descriptions (general, 44/5), IT (general, 48-75g), Daoloth, Render of Veils (463-2b), Yog-Sothoth (many titles, 274-4/56c) Also see Lovecraft.

This will certainly be most interesting for me. Sitting alone in this cell for the last few days – not talkative, these guards: I suppose I shouldn't be surprised... It's given me a chance to clear my head, to put the vast majority of my recent experiences into some kind of perspective.

Yes, I am a relatively well-educated man, Doctor Marshall, but don't let that fool you. Besides, look at you. You're the psychologist but, honestly, shouldn't I be the one who is nervous under these circumstances?

No, I'm not, but you are still missing the point. I know why you are.

Yes, alright, I will get on with the story. I realise now exactly how it sounds, how strange and almost laughable it may appear. But I assure you, this is what happened. And besides, you're not going to laugh, are you?

Ten months ago I was a successful programmer for an equally successful games developer. An interesting job and one which gave me access to some unusual programs. I also took a lot of drugs, mostly dope, Ecstasy, sometimes cocaine. A well-paid job, I should add. I went out clubbing a lot. But the combination of these things led to some strange events.

I would sit at my terminal, working from home, as ever, messing around on the Internet or getting wrecked and playing with fractals and assorted designs that I intended to include in my later work on the games products. All very enjoyable. I wasn't one of those techno-hippies though: the shamanistic tendencies, the revolution, none of that attracted me. Despite my club experiences, I spent most of my time there in chill-out rooms, watching colours and thinking about very little if I'm honest. I always assumed that most people did the same. It was a good feeling in general, I admit, but it would hardly induce any noticeable raising of the consciousness. Rather the opposite. Without some initial evangelical zeal or desire for spiritual feeling, I imagine we all looked like grinning fools.

I'm not losing you, am I? No, I gathered you had never done such things. It is... possibly... different here. But anyway, I did have ideas of my own.

I won't bore you with the technicalities; I imagine you have all my programs stored away.

Safely.

Do you want to know the trigger? Yes, I'm sure you do. Well, it's not hidden in any way. I called it Daoloth. For obvious reasons. I only called it that afterwards, of course, when I realised what it could do, or had done. I got the name from Lovecraft. No, you won't have heard of him, unless there are others in my situation. Which I very much doubt. Start a new file. I can tell you a lot. But all in good time.

One night I adapted a fractal creation program and introduced a chronological variable so that the structure could evolve over time. I had seen similar things done before and they had interested me from a design - a professional - point of view. It is fascinating, you know: great whirls of arbitrarily coloured substance, spots of darkness like abcesses, mouths, eyes, all coming and going, growing and coalescing at the same time, infinite and endless.

Absorbing.

Especially if you were under the influence of those great and glorious mind-expanding chemicals, as they used to be called. And naturally I was. I do remember a moment when it occurred to me that this was very like Lovecraft's description of Yog-Sothoth – yes, the same man. If you wait, it will all become clear in time - the All-In-One, a shapeless congeries of protoplasmic bubbles. Or was that the other thing? I don't remember precisely. Anyway, it was really very good. I must have fallen asleep or passed out while the program continued to run because I awoke to the screen blank and boring screen-savers running about. All very two-dimensional and prosaic by comparison.

Yes, Dr. Marshall, I did indeed dream. You don't miss a trick, do you? I can't imagine why you would be asking about my dreams. Come now, don't look so worried. I'm perfectly willing to tell you all I know.

The dream... well, look, I hesitate to call it that because at the time it was certainly more of a nightmare. Now I realise that, at the very least, it was a dream. Back then anyway. The fractal form spiralled over itself for hours. It took me that long to realise that it had spilled out of the screen and was churning up my view of the wall. I couldn't move. It

8

grew and grew and grew, expanding all the time, replicating infinite changes of self, reproducing whole worlds and devouring them in seconds. Soon I could see nothing else. Eventually I was swallowed by one of the mouths. Or noticed by one of the eyes. It amounts to the same thing. It still went on. I saw the same thing repeating itself but now I felt part of it, inside something. That is all.

Yes, certainly, the terror was enormous. I can't feel or describe that properly now. Do you really want me to? There are only my new words for it, the prayers, the invocations.

All right. For the record then.

The Ultimate, the construction of endlessness, *Iä Yog-Sothoth*, the mighty and visionary substance of Azathoth, the chaos of infinite replication, never-ending, always-changing, swallowed and regurgitated, destroyed and reborn, the originary finality of dimensional freedom, space and time consumed, the Way and the Gate, movement beyond space, happenings behind time, *Yngaiih, yngaiih, Iä Yog-Sothoth*, A different world.

Is that enough?

Doctor, in all seriousness, are you sure you wouldn't like to take a break?

Alright, if you insist. I'll continue.

The dream being over, I continued to work for some days. Then the visions began to creep up on me. At work, in the office, I mean, out of the corner of my eye, I would catch other screens filled with the chaos of my program. For a few seconds, I could even stare at the burgeoning void and then everything would return to normal. It frightened me for a time. The worst occurred when I went out that weekend. At the club in [deleted] I had taken a few trips and some other things to get me relaxed. In the dark light room, I was watching a video screen when I realised that my program was all around me. The strangest thing was my instant understanding that it had been like this for some time. It was as if I had

9

only just become properly aware of it. Tendrils and lines of shining force were reaching off the screen and caressing the walls and the other people there, sweeping right through them, encompassing the whole building. They were inside me, too, tracing the outline of each cell, reaching even further down, down into the sub-atomic, shaping the quantum structures of all substance and connecting everything with everything else.

It was too much for me. Even the thoughts, the awareness I had of this thing, was becoming the thing itself. I don't know what happened. I must have screamed and run out of the place like a madman. I would have looked such a fool, just another casualty caving in.

Outside the visions cleared for a while. I had almost reached home before my consciousness accessed them again. Sorry, yes, a computer metaphor seems appropriate. In the clouds trails of fractal shapes became visible. They glowed orange in the sickly streetlamp light. The darkness of shadows was alive with the writhing invisible potential at the centre of the Mandelbrot Set. As I struggled to get my key in the door, it seemed to be taken from me and the door was opened all in one insane movement that existed outside time. I was swept back and forth, I was in my room on the floor, laughing, then in the club, then on the doorstep once more, then in my earlier dream, then back and forth with such dizzying swiftness that I lost all sense of my own individuality. Everything existed as one.

Somehow I was... re-established. I hesitate to claim this as my own achievement. By then I felt altered. Drastically and fundamentally alerted to a new and severe development. I sat down with a cup of coffee and a cigarette to collect myself, an entirely appropriate phrase both then and now. I had seen new things, my awareness was now vastly different to that of my previous incarnation. Strangely, I felt I

10

had a name to put to the process I was undergoing or had undergone; Daoloth, the Render of Veils. I had been privileged to witness the presence and the processes of the Key and the Guardian of the Gate, Yog-Sothoth, the All-In-One, a sort of cosmic aleph, if you like.

I laughed out loud at the time despite my fears. It was Lovecraft, you see, it was all his stuff that shaped these hallucinations. It came as something of a relief to find even part of an explanation.

Lovecraft, yes, of course. Howard Phillips Lovecraft, a weird fiction writer from the early part of the twentieth century, famous for creating primal and original myth stories combining odd science with a positively blasphemous futility. A pulp horror writer. Not terribly successful in his day.

No, you won't find any reference to him. Let me finish.

Lots of other writers took up and expanded his work. Hundreds of stories were written; Howard, Smith. Lumley, Campbell, Copper, Wilson, even King. All were indebted and suitably respectful. I knew all this because I had written about him myself at University, much to the disdain of my tutors. There were, I noted early on, two types of story. The first was set in a world in which Lovecraft had actually existed. These were usually contemporary updates in which, at some portentous moment, the protagonist would turn to someone and ask, "Have you ever read Lovecraft?", a question followed by an elucidation similar to the one I have given you. The tales normally made him privy to arcane information which could only be put on paper as fiction but was, to those in the know, thinly-disguised fact or at least real myth.

The other type of story was set in a world where Lovecraft himself could not have existed because the monsters and legends he created were in fact true and existing, if not extant: the world, in this case, where Lovecraft's own stories were set.

My distinction was not perfect and certainly did not contain the full range of Lovecraftiana but it did make a certain sense. Daoloth, I remembered, was part of a Campbell story, something from *Revelations of Glaaki*, I think. Yog-Sothoth. Well, that was real Lovecraft, *Dunwich Horror* and all that.

So I went to my bookshelf to do some research.

I had no Lovecraft on my shelves. They hadn't been stolen, there was simply no space to be seen where I had left them. I simply had fewer books. There were only three or four Panther paperbacks anyway; I'd never gone for the Arkham House editions. That doesn't matter. They were not there. And, more importantly, it looked as if they had never been.

Out of the corner of my eye, I saw other eyes watching me.

Campbell's *Cold Print* had disappeared too. That had the Daoloth story in it. This was ridiculous. What else did I have? That Robert Howard collection... Yes, you will have heard of him perhaps, creator of Conan, I know. Anyway, I looked for *The Black Stone* and some others. They were no longer there. Other stories had taken their place. I was confused. I couldn't think of other references I would have to hand.

I sat down and lit another cigarette. By now my hands were shaking and the visions were pressing on my brain again. All in all I felt very odd. I felt as though he was slipping away from me or retreating into my own changed mind. It made me surprisingly sad. Then I remembered my own essay from University. In a flurry of paper and files – I was quite desperate by then – I sat down on the floor clutching eight sheets of typed script. The title page read 'The Influence of the Gothic Tradition on Early Pulp Fiction'.

This was not my title. Scanning the contents I discovered that the essay contained no reference to anyone called H. P. Lovecraft.

I sat still for a long time. My cigarette ignited some papers after a while so I calmly poured cold coffee over the flames. From where I sat in the debris of my room, I could just reach a cheap World Atlas. Once again I sat with it in my lap for a very long time before opening it. At the periphery of my vision the mouths of the gods laughed at me. Inside my skull their geometries shifted space and time. My fingers ran with coalescing globules as I turned to a map of North America. There, beneath my shifting, changed finger, was the town of Arkham on the east coast.

Shut up, Dr. Marshall! Do not interrupt me now. This is so very important. Innsmouth and Kingsport are long gone now. You destroyed them decades ago, didn't you? And the underwater city. And I know all about the secret bases in Antarctica. You will find R'lyeh soon enough. Or it will find you.

You see, it was all fiction to me. I sat there with my finger on the black dot called Arkham for I don't remember how long. This wasn't my home. This wasn't my world. This wasn't even my story. I had been shifted, transformed somehow, by the Daoloth program. I have since found that it exists here, too, but I had to give it that name myself because here, here, so few people have read the *Necronomicon*. Where I came from there were fragments of it in the cheapest paperback. Everyone knew about 'that which is dead'. Pathetic.

Even now it makes me smile to see how frightened you are by all this. Do you want me to quote you some more? A fragment of *Unausprechlichen Kulten* perhaps? Tell you stories of dear old Miskatonic University? This is why you think I am mad: because I know all this, because I found that here I could reconstruct rituals that invoke the Old Ones. Of course, initially I tried to use the program to get me home. But the visions simply increased in potency and I began to lose track of time. I was alone in my room for days, staring at infinity, trying to recover Lovecraft.

Eventually the gods smiled upon me and gave me a purpose. That was when I started the Daoloth/Yog-Sothoth group in [deleted]. It was undeniably easy. I began to enjoy the work. I was in contact with Cthulhu cults, Nyarlathotep worshippers, the whole gamut of so-called insane cultists. And I was laughing all the time because I knew I was completely sane. I knew what it all meant. I saw it all from a different perspective.

And then, of course, the Security Services caught up with me. I had been noticing other differences as I went along. The new Draconian policing, the Extremist Acts, the outlawing of unusual forms of religious observance. When the crackdown on drugs and parties happened, and there was no outcry from civil libertarians, I knew it was all coming together. It was time to act. When the news blackouts began last February, or at least when the media restrictions became common knowledge, then I began the sacrifices.

So that brings us up to date, I think. I can see you're sweating Doctor. Please, sit down and relax. There, that's better. Now tell me. Something has happened, hasn't it? How many dead so far? How many lost? How many are mad?

Interview terminated at 23.53. Dr. Marshall committed suicide in his car after leaving subject at 01.02. Subject is now uncommunicative and uncooperative. State authorises any and all means for extracting further information. Situation now critical.

INVESTIGATIONS

This thick and bloated beauty,
That blooms in the darkest places...

Enoch Soames,
Fungoids.

"Is it dangerous?"

"I don't know. Do you care?"

In a tiny, air-tight glass bottle, a smaller piece of grey fungus. Grof took the offering, looked past the other man at his untidy flat and wondered whether he was ready for another trip. Grof's rooms had seen far better days. Since he had moved in, they had decayed even further, well below the level at which any less confused character would have moved out. Grof, however, did not look the kind of man who cared about such things. Thin to the point of emaciation, the filthy jeans and t-shirt that he wore barely found any flesh on which to hang. He had a hunted and haunted look that exposed his obsessive experiments with hallucinogens to perfection.

"Eat it as soon as you open the bottle. The Doctor told me it has a tendency to deliquesce on exposure to air. Take the whole piece. Don't waste time trying to save any. It dissolves phenomenally fast."

The other man looked far healthier by comparison. Shorter by several inches, he was relaxed even in these repellent surroundings. He had provided Grof with drugs for some time now, building him up to a state of dependence that gave the smaller man an unconscious pleasure. This unpleasant fact showed itself in his face whether he liked it or not. Grof would not, and did not, notice these things any more.

"Thanks. Here, take the money. I'll try it this afternoon."

"I'll call round later if you want, just to check on you. Unusual stuff, you know."

Even Grof noticed this unlikely concern. He looked sharply at Lardner, noticing, perhaps for the first time, how well dressed he was for a hospital orderly. How could he afford such a new leather jacket, the newest haircut, the gold watch? Then the reason occurred to him and he floundered.

16

"Ok, if you like. Or I'll call you when it's over."

"Hey, yeah, alright. I work in a hospital ok? I treat you like we treat real patients. Don't look so miserable. Remember, have a good time."

He tapped the unlabelled jar before leaving, as if for luck. Grof could swear he was whistling as he strolled down the corridor. Lardner made the money he did from people like Grof. That was how you got on in this world, how you got to wear gold watches. He sat down and sighed. Try not to think too much. Now seemed as good a time as any.

He popped the top off the jar, shook out the lump of fungus and placed it on his tongue, all in one quick movement, well before he had time to consider what he was doing.

For a split second it smelt and tasted so thoroughly revolting that he thought he would throw it straight back up. Gross fumes seemed to rise directly into his brain. Tiny spores crawled down his throat. Then it was gone, the dissolution almost instantaneous. He could feel nothing in his mouth as his tongue gingerly worked its way around, hoping not to encounter some undissolved fragment of that foul taste. No, that was it. In his bewildered state he wondered whether that time had come when Lardner began to rip him off, passing him dull drugs until he was forced to go through the hell of finding another supply. Or paying Lardner more money.

When he stood up to get a drink, he realised that this was not the case at all.

It began with a kind of tunnel vision. Darkness encroached from the edges of the room. Not normal darkness like the coming of night, but a deep, negative space that consumed the corners of his eyes. He sat down again quickly. His body felt normal so far but his mind raced, terrifying him with the prospect of blindness. All the awful possibilities occurred in a short space of time.

17

Paranoid and shaking, he weathered the storm. When his body began to go limp, he lay down on the sticky remains of the couch. This is very fast, he thought. That simple idea managed to distract him from the fear of losing his sight. The growth of the dark continued inexorably. Soon he found himself staring through a pinhole into the ruins of his kitchen, out of a window, into the midday sun. Then even that was gone.

He had never experienced anything quite like this before. It still felt like an hallucination, he decided. He knew he was not truly blind. He was just in a dark place, a place without light. Except for the stars.

Ahead of him, tiny spots of light appeared. The harder he looked the more of them he could see. Despite this, they made very little impact on the vast black expanse. Space, whether intergalactic or merely interstellar, surrounded him. A sudden sickening sensation of falling drew his attention forward, where he could see an even darker space than the aether around him. A planet loomed. He began to feel such a piercing cold in the bones he could not see, that all the fears of sickness and decay came back to him. Yet it seemed impossible that anything could rot out here. Nothing could even live.

His invisible body swooped low over the planet. The grey-black ashen surface came into focus and, as his perspective improved, he saw fantastic sights. The planet was a city. Huge terraced towers ran up and down like mountain ranges, giving no impression of a level surface. Despite having no windows, Grof knew instinctively that they could only be habitations. Holes dotted the terraces. Sometimes he saw movement, but not before he was swept down the immense gullys like some plunging bird of prey. Eventually, when the stars behind him had become little more than a strip of vastly distant diamonds, he saw a river of deeper blackness running between the impossible buildings.

Then revelations came, as he plunged towards the thickening liquid, unfrozen by age or cold. Creatures flew alongside, observing him. He could feel the beat of their pale wings, hear a buzzing inside his head that he knew was a terrible communication, one he would never comprehend. Finally, as the stars disappeared behind him, he realised that one of them was his own lost midday sun.

*

"I want some more."

"Good. I can get it. I'm very near, in fact. I'll bring someone, the Doctor who gave the stuff to me. You'd like to meet him. Don't go anywhere."

Grof dropped the payphone without hanging it up. He stumbled up the stairs back to his rooms. His head pounded with the worst headache he could remember. His peripheral vision was still clouded with the dark but he had to have some more of the grey fungus. He was so distracted by his experience that he did not think it unusual when Lardner knocked on his door less than five minutes after his call. He was not surprised by the appearance of the Doctor either. It was as if they had been waiting.

Grof barely managed to let them in. Lardner caught him as he fell.

"Where have you been? What was it like?" asked the distinguished man who followed Lardner into the front room. Grof found himself sitting in a kitchen chair. Lardner was busying himself with something, floating around in the dark, peripheral space. The Doctor stood before him, questioning. A greying, handsome man of around sixty, he wore a brown overcoat and carried a traditional leather case. Grof felt he looked like a proper doctor, the right man to deal in fantastic drugs.

"The black planet; you've been there. It has found you."

"I want some more." Grof repeated lamely, not able to listen.

"Good, we shall go out and get you some. You only need to tell us the way. Relax. We will guide you."

Lardner finally sat down opposite the Doctor. They formed a triangle in Grof's unpleasant room. Lardner and the Doctor exchanged glances. One of them put something on the small table between them. Grof could not see what it was. There was a click. For a split second, Grof realised that it was far from over. Then the three men left on their journey.

*

Outside was an ancient city. It was dusk as they walked the broken cobbles of a steep, narrow street. Beyond the crumbling wall beside them, green domes and black towers slowly lit up as night came on. Grof led the way, as if he knew where to go, while Lardner and the Doctor walked behind him. None of them spoke. Grof felt, rather than heard, their suggestions on which turning to take. The headache was turning into something unmanageable. He tried not to think about it. They continued beneath towering churches, skirted overgrown orchards where small, unripe fruits fell soundlessly onto grass as they passed by. Pinnacled domes on pale buildings were behind them and before them.

When they began a steep climb, Grof looked up to see a wall of windows above him. A complex of buildings topped the headland and behind these, two of the black towers slowly disappeared as they mounted a flight of steps. They were not the hideous terraces of his previous vision but more like the spires of a cathedral, hemmed in by vast offices. Behind them, the city opened onto a sea of darkening red roofs, broken up by darker parks. Far below, at the bottom of the valley, a more normal river than the last one he had seen, complete with stone bridges and quiet, human traffic, flowed.

They wound their way up the hillside, mounting steps where necessary and negotiating sharp bends until they lost sight of all that was above them. Finally the Doctor indicated an alleyway partially covered over by scaffolding. Once they had passed underneath this, more cobbles led them to an imposing wooden door, flanked by brass plates. On closer inspection, the plates said nothing at all.

Grof looked around at his two companions. It was night. No lights could be seen in the building before them. It twisted up and back, becoming one with all the other houses on the slope. The Doctor indicated that he should knock. Lardner smiled encouragingly. Grof took the shining metal in his hand and let it fall. There was no sound. Behind him, the doctor told Lardner that they were in Prague.

The pain in Grof's head increased dramatically when the door was opened. Lardner grasped his wrists and held him upright in an awkward position. He could hear buzzing, faint and far away.

"Where is it? Is it here?" said one of the three to whoever had opened the door. No-one replied.

Once inside, a long hall stretched away to another set of double doors at the far end. To the left, an ornate spiral staircase allowed a view of the night sky through a tall window, where only the hillside should be. Lardner held Grof even tighter. The pain and the buzzing were leading him down the hall to the other doors. Before the group had stumbled more than three steps, a figure in a wheelchair emerged from under the stairs. He seemed old and pale in the inadequate light and his expression was such that it was evident he was not expecting or pleased to encounter them. He blocked their way.

"You are here then?" he enquired, looking the strange group over with an intense glare.

"The grey fungus. Do you have it here?" Grof pleaded. Lardner still held him, though he turned his head away from such pathetic pleading. The man in the wheelchair laughed out loud.

"Here? Well, perhaps, perhaps not. Follow me, I feel I must tell you something of it first." He set off toward the other doors. The unstable pair of Lardner and Grof followed, while the Doctor brought up the rear.

"Does your head hurt, young man? I would expect it does, but I doubt they told you about that, did they? You, sir, you look considerably stronger than this pitiful specimen, would you be so kind as to open the doors?"

Lardner looked back at the Doctor.

"Don't let go of him Lardner. I'll do it."

"I felt you might, good physician that you are." The man in the wheelchair smiled unpleasantly as the Doctor pushed past him to grasp the handles.

The final room -Grof felt sure he would be going no further- had been painted white but was lit by only a few candles in a huge candelabrum, hanging from the ceiling. The terracotta tiles of the floor showed ancient, unintelligible chalk marks of obscure occult use. A wall was given over to five great oak bookcases. A desk strewn with papers faced the one tall window that showed the city skyline in all its towered glory. The centrepiece of the room however, was a simple but immense wooden box. It stood on a crumbling altar of pink and white marble in the middle of the room and seemed the focus of all the half-erased chalk marks on the floor. Grof almost cried out when he saw it. He knew the pain would stop soon. He could barely hear the old man over the buzzing. With alarming swiftness, the wheelchair was in front of them again.

"In 1587, Rudolf II wanted to make the lakes of Stromovka more impressive. Being a monarch of grand design, in more ways than one, he began construction of a tunnel that would lead from the Vltava River straight through the hillside to feed his precious lakes. A feat of considerable engineering, I think you'll agree. Without entering into a long description of the technicalities, I would like to paraphrase from a pamphlet written some years later by a young man in the Golden Lane under the castle, an apprentice to one of the many alchemists that lived and worked there. It is called *Beasts Beyond Tolerance or Understanding* and tells, with debatable clarity, a story told by the tunnelers, later corroborated and further elaborated upon by some of his master's associates.

During the second month of tunneling, the workers found a shaft deep inside the hill. They would never have happened upon it had they not been taking the tunnel on a slight detour to avoid some particularly intransigent rock. This shaft, or fissure, was inside that rock itself. It led upward into darkness and downward into darkness. They had no idea how to proceed. The new tunnel was unconscionably rounded, bearing too much resemblance to an engineering skill well beyond their petty pick marks. They panicked and attempted to return, but in the confined space nothing was easy. The tunnel so far was no wider than three or four feet while the illumination and shoring work left much to be desired. Then the buzzing began, and the terrible smell that rose from the pit in front of them caused the first and nearest to faint, falling forward over the lip to his presumed death. There was no cry but the buzzing increased in volume. From here on the pamphlet admits to being, at best, mere hearsay, stories told over too much beer. It is said that the next man, a remarkably brave soul, obviously with no sense of smell, looked down after his fallen colleague. What he saw, rising up on membranous wings, caused him to scream, setting up insupportable echoes in the half-finished darkness. Three men lost their lives in the scramble back to the light, trampled underfoot by their friends and drowning in inches of water on the uneven stone floor.

This is as much as could be gleaned from the sharp end, as it were. The rest our apprentice wrote down secretly and contains what he learnt from the sorcerers and alchemists that he communed with in his everyday life.

Those terrified few that found their way back to the outside world discovered, incredibly for them, that Rudolf himself was waiting. Guards, and an elite of those infamous alchemists too, were ready for them at the exit, to threaten or bribe them all into secrecy. Then, eventually, after much undisclosed preparation, these newcomers, to a man, entered the tunnel.

Later, as it was described to our young author, a shrouded, moving object was removed, crated and shipped in secret back to the Hradcany Palace. The impossible fissure was blocked and forgotten by whatever means necessary. The tunnel was continued with only a minor alteration in direction. After that, and our fellow's literary indiscretion, the legend was effectively silenced in the way only a great monarch can know. The young author merely speculates, at no great length, on Rudolf's true motives for his tunnel.

Which brings us, with a minor gap of some four hundred years, up to date, does it not? The thing in the crate, the Intolerable Beast, is not the only one of its kind; a fact, Doctor, of which you are fully aware. How else could you have started these investigations? Or indeed tracked me down in this peculiar way. It has certainly not been in my possession for the entirety of its incarceration, despite my long life. It is a fungal life form, not even entirely of this present universe, as old books would have it... But I am wasting time. Indeed, I have said more than enough, more than I would have wished, I imagine. And your friend here is all but finished. Let him loose and I shall uncover the creature. We shall witness, in a sense, a meeting of minds."

The old man reached up to the iron catches on the crate. Hoary metal creaked as the side crashed down. Grof broke free of Lardner's hold and, astonished he could still stand, stumbled toward the thing in the box.

There was glass between them even then, an extra layer of protection had been added sometime in that last four hundred years but it was clear enough, even with age and thickness. Nothing could conceal the alien nature of the beast within. It stirred, floating, as Grof held out his hand. The buzzing in his head began to resolve itself into sounds he could begin to comprehend. When he finally fell against the cool glass, the pain in his head, unbearable for so long, went out like a light. A pink and grey body slid around in the ancient prison to raise one of its many articulated limbs and scratch feebly at the place where a human hand touched the glass. A shape, a grotesquely soft conjunction of wasp and crab, came into view for the shortest time. Grof closed his eyes when he saw the grey fungus growing between the folds of what passed for the Beast's head. This was what he needed. His own exhausted body fell against the Bohemian glass, while in his mind, he and the creature flying beside him dove into the black liquids of its home planet, out on the rim of the solar system.

*

"Is he dead?" Lardner asked.

25

The doctor reached under the ropes that bound Grof to the kitchen chair, feeling in vain for a pulse.

"Yes."

Lardner rose to his feet and stretched. Grof's rooms stank. It was already night outside. For seven hours he and the Doctor had been guiding the increasingly demented Grof on his visionary journey. It was tiring work. The Doctor did most of the talking, though Lardner's wrist ached from the notes he had to take. It seemed pointless as there was a tape recorder on the table with a stack of cassettes, which they had also used. The tapes were full of Grof's whispered, elaborate descriptions, broken up by painful groans. The Doctor's voice, when it cut in with a specific question or hint, was loud and shocking. Lardner walked around the dirty room that now stank of fresh sweat as well as older, more ingrained smells. He would be glad to leave town after this.

"Was he in Prague, like you said?"

"I believe so. It appears that is where the creature is being held. It told him a good deal more than the last connection we made. The tunnels, Rudolf, the timing; it all fits in with our other researches. It was clever of the Beast to make old Orne tell its story. I cannot imagine he will be appreciating the irony. It remains subtle and powerful, even now. More importantly, I am convinced that it wants me to find it."

"What about the old man? He keeps turning up."

"The Beast's current owner. Unfortunately, as a man of some occult means, he is sure to know we are coming for him. It will be extraordinarily difficult to remove the crate to another locale, though we may have to move faster than anticipated."

"Then you know who he is?"

"In Prague? He may be Josef Nadeh, formerly Simon or Jedediah Orne. But it could all have been a disguise, his wheelchair, the alley and so on. He could do that, as he knows we are coming. He would confuse both the vision and the communion itself, if he can. He could include much that would throw us off the track, within limits. His experiments with the creature are obvious. No, we will have to travel to Prague and try again. Proximity will bring better results. I need the creature alive. What little of the fungus we get back from these investigations is not nearly enough."

"We'd better get on with it then." finished Lardner.

The Doctor reached into his case and drew out the bone saw. The top of Grof's skull needed to be removed before they could harvest the fresh growths.

BENEATH THE BLACK TOWER

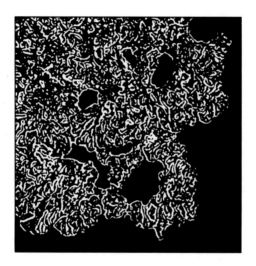

...an expedition which has never been popular, if only because we are obviously crushing half-armed and very brave men with the irresistible weapons of science.

The Spectator, 1904

May 4ᵗʰ 1904, Mission Compound Chang Lo, outside Gyantse, Tibet

"I did not see it myself but I am told, I believe truthfully, by the troops who discovered the room that it contained the bodies of men, women and children, all decapitated.

Other than that, and befitting my status as an Englishman – a *peling* to the Tibetans - in foreign climes, I must say that the weather has improved immeasurably since our arrival at Gyantse, as has our reception by the inhabitants of the town. A regular bazaar has set up outside the Chang Lo Mansion where we have made our headquarters and all manner of things can be purchased. A 'Mrs Wiggs', buxom, cheerful and local, has been running a vegetable patch very well for all of us.

It is a far cry from the events at Guru last month. The massacre there has caused consternation back home and we truly never expected to be made so welcome a month later and deeper into the country than ever. Here Doctor Waddell is busy curing Tibetans of various ailments, surprising them just as much as when he treated their surviving wounded after the battle.

All in all, the air is clearer. Still to hot or too cold and the national dress and habits of the Tibetans are still filthy in the extreme but otherwise we are in for a pleasant stay before the final push on to Lhasa, if Colonel Younghusband has his way.

The two remaining reporters from the Western papers are a little subdued. One of their number lost a hand in the fighting at Guru, an irony not lost on them. The soldiers laugh in their own way but they know this is not a true war or even an invasion. Colonel Younghusband's mission is simply to establish a meaningful relationship with the Tibetan government – before the Russians do, is the unspoken caveat. I have spoken with several of the officers. Many believe it is already too late. The

Dalai Lama (the thirteenth apparently) already has a Russian spy, an advisor or a chosen Lama at his side, depending on your point of view.

The only reminder of the antagonism we have faced and may face again is the overwhelming presence of the Fort on the cliffs above Gyantse town. It was taken without a fight; there were no soldiers to put up any defence in fact. But it is huge. A roomful of broken idols, a factory of sorts, apparently. And that place of decapitated bodies.

Perhaps we will never understand. I am going into the town this afternoon with a small escort, in search of enlightenment."

*

Kesang first saw the Englishman seated under a low tree away from the bright stalls of the bazaar. He was writing. The monk took this as a good sign. He had to, as there had been so few recently. He looked fit and healthy. He might survive.

He instructed his servant and the Nepalese interpreter to approach the man deferentially, with the offer of a pleasing story, something to take his mind off the recent fighting. Kesang watched them approach from a distance; saw the man start as if awoken from sleep. They were still nervous around Tibetans or anyone they didn't immediately recognise. They hid themselves away behind vast tents, any number of servants and pack animals. And, of course, their guns. They would never come into true contact with reality like that.

If they would not be warned, they would have to be shown.

In Gyantse, if the bait were taken, Kesang would drug the Englishman's tea. When he awoke, they would all be far away. He felt a degree of shame at his casual abuse of hospitality but he could think of no other path.

May 7th, elsewhere

"I am lost. Obviously I have no choice but to stay with Kesang and the others now. The interpreter, whose name as far as I can make out, is Ram, tells me that there is no need to fear. I beg to differ.

Ram and a young servant approached me yesterday with an invitation from a monk named Kesang. He was living in Gyantse at the moment and, if I were willing, he would be able to impart certain information that would be invaluable to the success of this mission, information that might bring about a positive outcome of some sort. Ram's abilities as an interpreter are not up to the task of communicating with precision.

I left the Mission in the early evening with several others but quickly slipped away, an easy task among the muddy tracks and single storey stone houses. I was foolish. Even then I saw new faces, angry, peering from windows. 'Mrs Wiggs' had not appeared that day. The walking wounded from the hospital had all left. I should have understood.

Kesang greeted me cordially. His house was surprisingly well appointed by Tibetan standards. The room we took tea in was even warm and comfortable, in high contrast to the muddy cold of the streets outside, peppered with dogs and dung. I insisted on taking the tea entirely black, without the rancid butter the locals consistently add. He smiled as I waved my hand ineffectually.

"You do not like Tibetan food?" enquired Ram, presumably on Kesang's behalf.

"On the contrary, I find it refreshing and simple. Uncomplicated." I looked from Ram to Kesang. The one babbled; the other nodded approvingly. Kesang was an unusual man by the standards of most Tibetan monks I had seen. He wore the traditional robes but had none of the self-absorption of others we had seen on the way into the country. Nor any of the foolish fanaticism that had led so many of them to fall before the guns. When he smiled I imagined I saw pain hidden somewhere, a distress unvoiced. I am sorry to say that he took me in completely. I had every desire to hear his tale.

The servant brought *tsampa*. While we ate, Ram asked what I thought of the country. When I hesitated, Kesang smiled and spoke directly to me. I continued to stare at the bald monk as Ram translated in my ear.

"It is clear you are unsure of your place here. It is difficult to form understanding. You, your people, grow outwards, up from India, you come to meet us, perhaps not in the best way. Perhaps we receive you the same. But so, even here, the world changes. The unknown becomes known. It is not always for the best."

Out in the street a dog howled. Others joined in. I imagine I heard screams. Kesang closed his eyes and began to chant an interminable mantra. I felt dizzy, strangely exultant. Sleep was coming. Ram reached out and took me in his arms before I fell. Kesang's prayer became a lullaby my Mother once sang to me. Then I was gone."

*

Kesang smuggled the Englishman out of Gyantse the same night, under cover of the attack. Ram and the servant followed them with three mules and enough provisions for a journey of several weeks. The lama did not wait to see the outcome of the violence. Men would assault the Mission and re-occupy the Fort. Many would die. Nothing would come of it. Kesang was not one of the ignorant. He knew when charms against bullets were useless. Only grief would come of such obstinate militancy.

When he awoke the *peling* was frightened. All the violence of his days welled up in him again. Kesang realised he was talking about his uselessness as a hostage, that the Expeditionary Force barely even knew he was there, how he had no influence with Colonel Younghusband or Brigadier General Macdonald, commander of the military escort.

By then they were miles from Gyantse, passing through ascending valleys of sharp black rock and twisted rhododendron. The streams were bright and pure. Above them white peaks and blue sky emphasised the intense clarity of the landscape. Kesang, failing to listen to the incomprehensible chatter for a moment, wondered if he would ever see the sacred lake Mansarovar again. He missed its massive still surface, reflecting the vastness above. He had made pilgrimages to many of the sacred places. He knew there were others, less still, hiding less acceptable wisdom. He held up his hand. The Englishman stopped rambling. Between Kesang, through Ram, to the disorientated, unwilling traveller, words resembling these passed.

"I am taking you on a pilgrimage. This is not a simple country. It has more than one name. It has more than one God. It has many more Demons. All of this you do not accept. I understand that you attempt acceptance. You try to seek out our places, understand our devotions. But the mandala is vast, the meditation never-ending. Here, we protect, we enshrine and therefore we must keep secrets. I would show you that which we hide. I will bring you to Leng and show you the Tower there. It is not for outsiders. It is not for anyone in truth, but it has been our burden. I regret my actions. I apologise to you now. But others would not do as I can do. You may succeed in reaching Lhasa with guns and soldiers but our rulers will not speak of this even then. And no good can come of that."

May 7th, night, beneath the mountain passes

"They all sleep so soundly, the three of them. It occurs to me that I have not even asked the servants name. Is this very British of me? And should I be more of a soldier? Sneak up on Kesang, steal a dagger, hold it to someone's throat and demand to be returned to the Compound? I would certainly have done such a thing earlier but we have spent hours riding and walking together. Kesang has tried to explain to me what he is doing in so many different ways. All in all, I am no longer frightened by him or by these circumstances. He has, in any case, promised to return me to the Expeditionary Force as soon as he is able. I find we are both in agreement about the attack on Chang Lo. Though neither of us saw it, it is futile.

That is not to say I understand him. As far as I can gather, he is some kind of rare warrior-monk, not trained to fight or provoke hostility in the peasantry like the ill-equipped men we have massacred so well on our way here, but to protect or defend something. It seems he must prove to me that it is against our best interests, apparently the world's best interests, to interfere in this strange country, which he now calls Leng rather than Tibet. I am unclear whether this is a region or another place altogether.

I do not understand. Kesang is forceful but apologetic around me. Ram is an unknown quantity. He seems to resent Kesang and is secretive about his loyalties. The monk is oblivious to all this. Perhaps I have more in common with the servant now. I will ask his name tomorrow."

*

Kesang cannot allow Ram to accompany them on the final approach. They must split up. Ram and the servant are to go on to a safe village hidden in a valley four miles to the east. Kesang and the *peling* must continue alone. It is extremely cold. The monk has brought sufficient clothing for his companion. Aside from his height he may not be noticed as a foreigner, muffled under yak skin cloaks and woollen scarves. As they part, Kesang notes the look of envy that Ram gives them. Ram is a fool. So many have fallen that way. Misunderstood the power.

When they reach the head of the first pass, he stops at a *Chorten* and, as the *peling* stamps about to keep warm, he prays, repeating the entry mantra. The Tower of Leng is very far. Walking will not take you there, only devotion. He has tried to explain as much to the Englishman but Ram's abilities had faltered. His choice had been a good one though. The Englishman helped him to his feet and when he looked in his eyes he saw a kind of comprehension.

"We must go on. Only hours now, only time. You will feel the place change," he said. They both grinned beneath their scarves.

May? Returning from the Tower

"Vile practices. Kesang could do nothing for me. Trying to force some explanation out of him I almost became violent, but it was useless. He just repeated words I could not understand. What happened?

We climbed higher and higher into the mountains. For the best part of the day snow was all around us. Then on some high ridge, Kesang made us stop. He pointed ahead. Within minutes the clouds parted and a deep valley could be seen. At the far end a massive vertical strip of black rock emerged from a white mountainside, looking for all

36

the world like a tower of ebony. I took in the strange view as well as I could but he continued stabbing his mitten at the place so I should look harder. Finally I noticed caves in the summit with exposed stairs clinging to the rock face. As I followed them down to their lowest point – three hundred, four hundred feet below? – I saw indistinct outlines of snow-covered structures leading away, all in a row, down through the valley, toward the ridge on which we perched. The closest was perhaps half a mile distant, down in the valley. I grasped his arm, indicating that I wished to see it. He did not want to descend. I can only assume he thought it too dangerous. I cannot see why. It is what has finally convinced me of his good intentions.

It was a hard descent. The snow was treacherous and the wind blew the mist around us like prayer flags to a huge god. I was the first to reach it. Twisted wooden poles held a rope net four feet off the ground, less than three above the snow. I looked underneath.

Red ice.

Kesang shouted something to me but I ignored him. On the top, I attempted to brush off the thick layer of snow. More black and red. Something frozen solid. Kesang put his hand on my shoulder. I shook the net, pulled on the rope where it was attached to the pole nearest to me. I became frantic. It was old, how old I wonder now? Then it came away, spilling snow and its contents at my feet.

Three naked human bodies, frozen together, their hands bound above their heads. Worse, if possible, than this – the chests opened like doors and nothing inside but snow.

The world became silent. I found myself wanting to scoop snow from the cavities, searching for the obviously missing organs. I turned to face Kesang. Once more, like some stage magician, he swept his arm along the valley. The mist cleared and

37

I saw dozens, perhaps hundreds, of these awful podia, leading the way up to the black tower.

I held his padded arms and shook him. More snow blew up around us. Was it tainted? Coloured pink, black, with blood? We were both shouting. Neither of us telling the other anything they couldn't already see.

And so I have seen evidence of cannibalism, the devouring of corpses to be precise.

It took us hours to get away from the tower. There was no need to speak. Kesang tried occasionally but I was not listening. After my initial horror came memories of all the history of British disgust at our discoveries; the Thuggees, Kali-Worshippers, bloody idols, Tantra, all the things those poor journalists back at the Compound delighted in titillating the masses with back home. First hand, it overwhelmed me. Before we got back to Ram I tried to tell Kesang that I understood. That I am grateful for this warning he has given to the Empire and to me. I do not want Ram to hear this.

It is getting dark now. We arrived in good time but the village appears to be deserted. Kesang is rushing about like a mad thing, seemingly more concerned now than ever. Something is wrong. Again, just when I think I understand...

Ram has spoken to me. Kesang stopped his frenzied packing to watch us as he crouched down.

"Did you see it?" he asked.

"What?" I replied. I felt the urge to back away from him.

"The Black Tower. Tell me, what is it like?" He sounded pitifully excited.

Kesang has

*

Kesang knows now that he has failed. The Englishman is so taken up with the external practice that he cannot see deeper. He barely saw

38

the Tower at all, he could not feel the darkness beneath it, feel the presence of the thing that should not be. Outsiders cannot easily penetrate the veil of substance. And the village – empty. There should have been dozens of friends here, ready to re-equip them for the return journey. Now it would be more difficult.

The Englishman is trying to thank him. Kesang does not want this. He has been misunderstood. It is worse, much worse, than the outsider could possibly imagine. At least, as Kesang packs what little they have, the Englishman writes again, preserving something. Then a further calamity occurs to him. Perhaps he has only made things worse. The Westerners will come now with their guns and machines in an attempt to purge this place in their blind revulsion. Untold damage will be done. There can be no victory here, only continued, ever-lasting struggle.

He turns as Ram crosses to the Englishman. They talk. It is a pity, for the monk knows that Ram's own mouth has nothing to give but dung. The Englishman is sitting under a tree again, writing. Suddenly it is as if they had never met. The monk wishes it were so easy to undo actions. But the wheel never stops.

Then Ram is shot through the heart. He falls backward.

Another rifle from out of the twilight ruins the Englishman's arm as he reaches forward to help the already dead interpreter.

Kesang is too far away to help them. He may not have been seen yet. He hopes the servant will stay in the houses he has been searching. They must hide. Calmly he leads the loaded mule into the darkness where he will not be found. No good will ever come here now. The Black Tower reaches too far.

The Tower

"It is over. We are at the end. Nothing has happened to me.

This will be my last entry - what else can I do but write? My other arm is useless. They wash it but will not bind it in any way. The blood... I must concentrate.

Ram was killed as he left me. Then I was shot in the left arm. Kesang disappeared into the night. God knows where the servant (who?) had gone. I went toward Ram's body in the hope of finding a weapon but the pain slowed me. The men came out of the darkness when I fell.

They are short, massively built beasts – perhaps I shall refuse to call them men – swathed as ever in furs and wool but with the addition of bones and skulls as adornments. None are recognisably human. They all wear a basalt pendant around their necks, of no consistent shape but blacker than hell itself. I imagine it is of the same stone as the Tower itself. I doubt they speak any dialect of Tibetan I have ever encountered. There were twelve of them in the raiding party. They shouted and laughed amongst themselves. I made no effort to communicate, as there seemed little point. We waited while some searched the village for Kesang. They returned empty handed. I must say I was pleased. In fact I laughed. They shouted at me.

We began my second trip to the Black Tower.

At night the trip felt different, somehow shorter and less arduous. I covered my arm as much as possible with the furs I wore. The cold helped to numb the pain as well. Strangely, they gave me my diary and pens, forcing them into my pack when I would not help them. They took no torches, no lights of any kind. Snow in darkness is an extraordinary thing. Is the vision black or white?

The wind had dropped as we descended the slope that I knew to be the last approach to the

Tower, the valley of the corpses. We used them as guides, walking beside the ghastly things along the valley floor. I counted forty-five podia before I collapsed. So many bodies. Looking up at the sky I realised there were no stars. Nothing at all. Only black.

When I regained consciousness I looked out over a precipitous drop. I was being carried up the stairs on the outside of the outcrop of rock that looks so much like a tower. Close up it is more obviously a natural, if unusual, phenomenon, sheer enough for snow to fall past it. Overhangs keep the steps clear for most of the way up. When we reached one of the caves we entered a tunnel. I cannot say, from here on in, what may be natural or unnatural. As before, I refuse to use the term 'man-made'.

There were others in the tunnels. We seemed to continue upwards. Words were exchanged. Shouts in the darkness. There must have been a hall of some sort, large enough to support echoes but I could not see clearly. Eventually, I was taken before an old man. The fact that his eyes were completely black, as black as the walls, could no longer come as a surprise. I saw this when the first torches were lit. I was being exhibited; a decision was to be made.

The old man tore off my head coverings and I realised that it was not cold in here at all. I remember the surprise overcame my fear for a short time. I found myself to be somewhat hysterical, as I had been at the village. Next he pawed at my wound, unwrapping what little bandage I had created. There needed to be an opening, and blood perhaps.

If I could remember a time when I was... if I could think, imagine, back to before, how afraid I was, when I swore, prayed to a God. If I could remember that now... too much effort. The story goes on.

41

The last room in which I ever truly existed was in the top of that tower.

A door was opened in front of me. I thought of the room in the Fort at Gyantse, filled with headless bodies. If only it had been that simple. This space was only fifteen feet square, the walls of that hateful black rock, the ceiling, domed and shadowed. Steep awkward steps, not cut for any human use, led down from all four walls to a central square, five feet below the doorway. This small flat surface was covered with an intricate sand mandala. I have seen these before. Monks take many days trickling coloured sands into these complex designs. Buddhist demons line the edges, living in castles and flowers of bright geometric colour. Tracks, dots, patterns of every sort are ritually laid out in pre-ordained order. Meditation on these images can lead to... what? I have never known. I will never know. I am no longer a part of it. The mandala is the world. Everything is in it. It is in everything. And in this one there is a black hole at the centre.

A space for nothing.

They would not push me in as I could have fallen down the steps. Instead a knife in my back prodded me forward. One deep step down. The door shut silently behind me.

I wonder how long it took. There is no night any more, no day. I am part of nothing else, nothing is part of me.

I sat as best I could on the top step, not wishing to move far from the only possible exit. Muffled chanting began outside the door. Beyond the thin air, triggered by some alien necromancy, barely perceptible movements began. The patterns rose gently from the lower floor, swaying rhythmically to a beat I could not sense. Perhaps, I imagined, these were living things, dancing to the music of other gods, the demons of another pantheon in flight. I imagined many things before...

I no longer know anything. Any of my fruitless conjectures back then may be true. None of it matters. In the end, whatever they were, they all fled before that which crawled up from the hole.

I was not so privileged.

Blackness. A thing that should not be. Something from far outside the mud walls of our very existence. Coiling sinuous ropes of ebon smoke, soft as hair, intractable as time, insinuating themselves into every pattern and flower. And, eventually, into me.

In the end, nothing is here.

I was screaming all the while. I could sense its dark negative presence all too clearly. Alone and mad. We were trapped here alone. A smoke tendril ran up my arm to the wound and dove in. I saw it, felt it move through the universe as the mandala, the world, coalesced into some form that drew away from me, spinning into the infinite distance. The world has been taken from me.

We were alone together. We are one.

But we are nothing.

So I am nothing now."

*

The village had been attacked. The raids had not abated, though Kesang had been told otherwise before he left Gyantse. There was always need of fresh sacrifices on both sides. Leng had reached out a dark paw and taken many. The survivors, hardy but surprised and saddened, found Kesang and the servant in the early hours of the morning. They lodged in a small *lhakang* high on a mountainside. First they prayed together. Then the monk explained what he had tried to do with the outsider and, in the end, how he had failed.

A hermit, who had lived in the caves behind the building for longer than anyone could remember, when asked the proper question, told them that the man still lived. Kesang became desperate. If he lived he could be rescued. The hermit shook his head, blind eyes seeing further than ever. Kesang must not be led astray in this. He should not be blinded by mistakes. The other man lives, but he does not truly exist any longer, said the hermit. He is gone. There are things that should not be.

Kesang argued. He pleaded and begged. The hermit only returned to his endless chanting.

Reluctantly the man who had become leader of the villagers after the raid suggested that arrangements could be made. It had always been like this. The monks like Kesang and others held Leng and the Black Tower in check, negotiated its very existence and kept it hidden, far from prying eyes. And in return, the Black Tower took lives. Some said it was not meant to be in the world at all. It had been this way for thousands of years, perhaps as long as the Black Lodge had fought the White. The only possible effort was to maintain that ancient balance. This was, Kesang argued, all he had been trying to do. But he had overestimated the Englishman's ability to comprehend. The *peling* could not, in the end, take back a warning that would be heeded by others like him.

Unless he himself had become that warning.

Kesang considered this.

Three days later, at the foot of the Black Tower, Kesang and two others watched the Men of Leng throw the Englishmen from a cave mouth high above them.

It was a fine, clear day, and free of falling snow or tearing winds. He fell slowly, like a black star through a white night, trailing darkness behind him like smoke. His pack was thrown after him though it hit the ground first. The two men with Kesang, warriors but unversed in the subtleties of

Leng, cried out: this was not what had been agreed; he was to be returned alive. Kesang held up his hand to silence their ignorance.

The body landed as lightly as a fallen leaf, still raising a plume of white snow around it. Kesang approached and looked down, fingering his prayer wheel and mumbling. The Englishman had not been harmed by the fall. His clothing was falling off him, turned to rotten rags. The wounded arm was black to the shoulder, ridged like the rock of the tower. Even in the harsh daylight shadows, a solid darkness played constantly in and over his skin, sometimes like water, sometimes like the wings of a great insect. His eyes, when he opened them, lifting his head to look at the monk, were black. He did not speak.

Kesang continued to pray as he lifted the man onto the stretcher they had brought. He watched the face, looking for some sign of recognition, of sanity. The black orbs stared back, unblinking.

His condition deteriorated quickly on the journey toward Lhasa. Sometimes his limbs would pass through the restraints and he would fall from the stretcher, sinking far into the snow. The black affliction on his arm spread to his entire left side. His face became sorely disfigured. The original wound had no more substance now than a faint shadow.

There was no communication. Every morning, Kesang would pray aloud as the fading body lay propped against a rock. Once, four days journey from the Holy City, Kesang thought to pass over the diary and pen still in the Englishman's pack. For the first time the ruined face looked away from the monk and down at the book. A shadow of an arm lifted the pen.

"Begins to work, then wheels turn. Even though I could not exist, I try. Undefined. Lost.

45

Darkness is sweeter than earth's red wine. Leaving this place. I have been shown the centre of things. Nothing is there. Nothing to see. I cannot continue here. Dissolved in the tide, no one will listen. Silence and darkness our only heritage. Everything is leaving me."

*

A day later the body fell from the stretcher and could not be lifted. The limbs, black but insubstantial now, passed through Kesang's gloved hands. The weather had turned bitter again. In the night, as snow began to fall, a silent vigil was kept by the three men. The white flakes settled for a moment on the darkness and then passed through. A drift slowly formed beneath the body until only an outline could be seen. Then the wind took the shadow away.

Kesang kept the diary. Later, in Lhasa, he learned that a compromise had been reached between the British and the acting Tibetan Government. Though the Dalai Lama had fled with his Russian advisor, Colonel Younghusband, the Chinese ambassador, the Regent and the senior Abbots had all signed a successful and balanced agreement. After so much fighting, Kesang, like many others, was amazed. The universe moved forward. Kesang, choosing to see wisdom over madness in the last diary entry, decided on retreat from it.

Before his last pilgrimage, to leave this world as a hermit, Kesang performed his final task. Discreetly, and without any hint as to its contents, he passed the diary on to the British forces, letting karma take its course. The British, blundering, arrogant but perhaps equally discreet, lost it amongst the vast acres of paperwork that ran the

Empire. No one, it seemed, could remember who the author had been.

Nothing is everywhere.

*

"The *dzong*, which is half ruined, is built tier upon tier to the summit of the steep rock...Went right to the top. There are no staircases, so we had to pull the ladder up from roof to roof. In a tiny dark room at the very top sat a monk, muffled up in a heavy red cape, beating a huge gong and praying to the spirit of the *dzong*. He seemed to be in a trance and appeared quite oblivious of our presence. I felt an unaccountable terror as if in the presence of something deeply sinister."

Spenser Chapman,
Lhasa: The Holy City, 1939.

AMONG THE PAVILIONS OF THE GREAT KHAN

With Indian tea in a Prague café, waiting for an American student to bring him stolen Hungarian antiquities. Even in the face of almost total financial collapse and professional isolation, he still imagined this was a suitable place for international research. Then, downstairs, a nightclub called The Whole of the Law began to throb, practising for the weekend. He sighed and put away his notes. This was no place for a real academic. His ears hurt just imagining how loud it would be down there. Outside, snow fell for the third time that week. Soon, a bitter winter would be upon Czech capital. No surprise or concern to the inhabitants certainly, but a nagging worry for a man previously used to heated rooms in Cambridge. Now he had barely enough money for another few days in a terrible hotel. And how much would these papers cost him? What few negotiations there had been were short and equivocal. He looked at the door. Would the student even show up?

To anyone else, this would have been a relatively minor concern. After all, he had discovered other things to worry about. But the tea was still hot and behind the clouds the sun still shone. Cars drove by outside. The blood of millions no longer flavoured the earth. He would not think that way for the moment.

"But you're famous," said the student, shaking off snow from an entirely inadequate coat, "I looked you up on the internet. You're a professor. Why couldn't you get this stuff yourself?"

Famous? That's what you get for using the internet as a reliable source of information, he thought. Look deeper; that was what he had always told his students. Never rely on the surface. Use the surface to take you below, into the undercurrents of history. Where the real thing happens. Of course, it was all nonsense: calculated tomfoolery to get them off their backsides and into primary sources, archives and the like, rather than relying on a confection of tertiary books by second-rate authors. And, of course, the damned internet.

And where had this got him? What happened if you did dig deeper? What would you find out about me, about the world? Not worth comment.

"Do you have the papers?"

"Yes. It was quite easy really. They can't be all that important. What's the deal?"

"Five hundred dollars,"

The student smiled and relaxed. "Yeah, I know that. I meant, what is the deal with you and the papers? Come on, tell me. There's nothing in them really."

Oh for God's sake, he thought angrily, you can't have read them, let alone understood what they might mean. Why assume so much just because they're in some out of the way archive at Charles University? He had nothing to go back to. He had been suspended from Cambridge over a year ago, without pay. A breakdown, of sorts, had consumed him for over a month soon after. His wife was long gone, even before this. He stared over the table at the tanned young man and thought of the cold outside. It made him angry, as so many things seemed to do these days. What would you know?

Hungary was devastated. The populace stood in shuddering groups at the edges of cold forests, watching the burning remains of their cities and towns go dark into the nights. Those that survived, weeping in the ruins of the aftermath, were further stunned by the sudden disappearance of their destroyers. In the spring of 1242 they left, as swiftly and efficiently as they arrived. This was like nothing Europe had ever seen. Where was the victory in this? Where were the victors? What, in the end, was the point? Why had God made such men?

In the beginning one of the many terrible surprises had been an English ambassador from the

51

invaders, delivering an ultimatum that would brook no debate, let alone opposition. No negotiation? No valour, no chivalry? A million dog-headed Tartars; everywhere at once. The massacre of thousands, even after surrender? After the debacle of the Crusades the West could waste no time debating the nature of Christian charity. So why had this alien people invaded, plundered and disappeared? How did one Englishman come to speak for them?

Most never discovered that, far away in the East, Ogodai, the Great Khan, had died. The succession was in question once again. All must return. The conquests, the empire, didn't matter. There was always China. Europe, whatever that was, could wait. The despoilers of the land left, leaving only corpses and questions behind them. Men need answers but they do not always wish to hear.

Realistically, the Mongols retreat was not always so sudden or efficient. What was left of a troop of Hungarian nobility, previously in ignominious flight, sleeping in woods, filthy and defeated, came upon a final group of horsemen in preparation for a delayed departure. They did not enquire what argument, failure or loss had slowed their leave-taking. Instead they fell upon them with all the arrogant bravado and terrified vengefulness of a lost cause. And triumphed, if they could be said to remember such a feeling.

The horses eyed each other with suspicion. Even they knew that they had come from different worlds. The Western steeds, tall, bloodied, starving and few in number, may as well have been another race. The Mongol horses sniffed around their dead comrades, five down, sixteen stamping, strangely nervous of blood, remembering the open steppe. This was an unlikely situation. To be taken so easily was a betrayal of all the Mongols held dear. Anger held sway on both sides.

But there was blind luck involved here too. Before all the Mongols were put to the sword, there was an ill-accented cry in Latin. That Englishman's name, the one who had delivered the ultimatum only months before, stayed the hand of a tired and hysterical Hungarian soldier.

"Speak."

"I know him. I know of you. I speak your language."

"Why? How?"

"He taught me. I was to be a Shaman. He wanted to know me."

It was enough to save him. Later, in a rude camp, a priest, when one could be found, interrogated the Mongol. The priest was tired. He understood no more than the soldiers but he continued to question and had made his ignorance a virtue. Mysterious ways, he had repeated to himself in the dark days, the Lord moves no matter what. Mysterious ways.

And so the Mongol, who should have lived, told his story to the priest, who should have died.

While at the same time, not so far away, at Wiener Neustadt in Austria, a similar interview was taking place. The Englishman himself had been captured during a final, exploratory and, he must have thought, largely pointless raid into Austria.

His world had ended now. All his life, a life of running further and further into the savage East, was over. Only torture and death stood between him and judgement. He said as much to Father Yvo, the priest sent to interview this alien emissary of the Anti-Christ. He had much to say, in fact. Father Yvo, like the other priest, was horrified by his experiences and would not listen to all his tales, designed, as they may have been, to increase that time before death. The torture, he knew, happened regardless. It was a necessary adjunct to the proceedings. No one would believe he spoke the truth otherwise.

So two priests listened to two confessions and out of them rose another tale, more threatening and more fantastic than anything they had heard before.

The Englishman had been at the *kuriltai*, the Great Meeting, in 1235. It was here that the expansion into Eastern Europe was proposed and decided. His advantage, his passport in this new world, was a knack for languages. The Khan's court was as international as Venice, in its own way. The Great Khan surrounded himself with clever men, men he could use in the furtherance of his conquests. One of these was Yeliu Chu-Tsai, a Chinese, who had been Genghis Khan's chancellor. He now gave Ogodai guidance on the future. He had been advisor to the Khans for many years and knew the feel of change. The Englishman found himself summoned to an audience with the Chancellor when the sun was high. The Mongols slept off their drinking of the night before. These two men knew when to talk and in which language. Both were alien here. Both survived well.

"So, you will be used a great deal in the West."

"Of course, Chancellor."

"How far will you go?"

"I do not understand."

"Indeed. I am not surprised, as I have asked too many questions in one." Refreshments were taken. The ageing Chancellor rearranged his seating. The tent was warm. The Englishman began to sweat. He did not like the thought of subterfuge. He did not like the thought of returning to the West. He wanted the simple life, of taking and following orders, no matter how brutal. He wished he could sit.

"Sit then," said Yeliu, "if you must. I am an old man now. I have had influence over the Khan for many years. I believe I have guided him well. We have won many victories."

"The blood of our enemies leaves many fertile lands," rejoined the Englishman, attempting to show his support of the wily old man.

"Blood, yes. I have saved many lives too." The Englishman said nothing. "Do you know of Badu Khan, cousin of our Great Khan?"

"Yes, Chancellor."

"He has been in Tibet."

"Yes."

"He has been making arrangements with strange authorities there. He has been involving himself in otherworldly affairs." The Englishman was, by now, truly uncomfortable. Successfully avoiding any talk of religion or superstition had become second nature to him, so much so that he did not think on it any more. He had been hounded out of England, then driven from the company of prim and priggish knights into the surprisingly welcoming arms of the 'cannibal Tartars'. His own beliefs had been destroyed in the Holy Lands and he felt no desire to reflect on what might come to replace them in this heathen place. Mongol worship was a private, personal thing. The Shamans led tribes to victory, food, shelter. He shut his eyes to more complex issues. He believed nothing.

"I shall tell you a story. You must take from it what you will. That is the simplest way." The Englishman remembered he was in the middle of a massive gathering of Mongols, all alive with the success of conquest, every one of them brought up, rooted, in the belief that the World belonged to them and their leader. Everyone else was servant, slave or dead. He could not escape. There was nowhere to escape to; the Mongols had conquered half the World already. They were truly a force of nature.

"In the mountains of Tibet, there is a door. Through that door, there is a place of power. It is a Black Tower on a dark mountain that is, and has been, for longer than life itself, a Monastery. Worshippers, not human, not alive in any sense you or I might know, have waited there, conducting themselves according to unseen laws. There is a balance to the world, as the Tao is seen simply. This remains a part of that, though this place is," here he smiled without humour, "the weightier part of the balance. There is a hole there. Beneath the Black Tower is a space of nothing, a devouring, unending, perhaps even inevitable thing. They call it, without foolishness, a creature that has no name. It reaches out beneath the earth and blood feeds it.

I have seen emissaries from the Black Tower here. The Great Khan is listening to proposals from Badu. The blood spilt has awoken their interest. The balance tips. The time may come when we do the work of a greater and infinitely more terrible master. The Great Khan may fall and I fear it would be better to die." The Chancellor became irritated when the Englishman turned his face away and did not respond. "Yes, I am an old man and I have many ways to fear death. But do not mistake me. I have seen this World for many years. I have seen the changes. I know more things now than I would ever have wished as a young man. But there is no going back. Except for you."

The Englishman had not understood more than half of this veiled circumspection. But it came from Yeliu, the Grand Chancellor, and was being told to him, the only man from the West in a thousand miles. The old man's conduct, the quiet around them, emphasised the only important element of the meeting: a warning.

"I am to die?" asked the captured Mongol, showing neither fear nor any real interest.
"Of course,"
"Then I will tell you how it came to be that the Englishman knew me and of what we saw together. You will kill me quickly for this?"

"Yes."

"I do not know your world," the Mongol began, "But the Englishman told me he had fallen as I had, and fallen far. He was happy to be at one with his enemies. But he would fall again, still further, into the very abyss, he claimed, if he did not share what he had seen. Every life counts. This is what I know. Every single one. A barrel of blood, that is what we are. A barrel of blood.

"I do not know why he confided in me. Perhaps it was because I had failed as a Shaman in my early years. He recognised something of himself. We had both fallen. He said that he dreamed. He dreamed of darkness and blood. His days were filled with death; his nights, he claimed, were worse, filled with more than death. Then, not long ago, after we had killed the peasants here..."

"The massacre in the valley? After you gave the people seed and horses to grow crops again in exchange for their women, sisters, mothers, children?"

"Yes, then."

"Oh Lord, have you no words? They were killed, stripped naked and massacred after they had worked and done as you said and given themselves to you and still you killed them all. Every one."

"Yes. Their blood in the ground. Every life counts."

"Lord help me. Continue."

"He was injured in the fighting before this. An arrow pierced his arm and he fell to the ground. Blood touched the earth and he shook like a leaf in the wind. When he awoke he told me of a carved black stone in the hills nearby, an ancient portal, a doorway. He said some terrible thing had found him, taken his soul away with it, beneath the earth, far away. His wound had gone bad. His nightmares consumed him like a sickness. One day, on the hill, as they died beneath us, he clutched at me and begged for help. He asked me if it was better to die

57

but I could not answer. Then show me, he cried out, show me.

I believed I had understood. So I stole herbs from a true Shaman, found what I could in this strange land. I sent the others away at his hoarse demand and closed the tent up. I practised what I remembered of the dances and the fires. The smoke burnt our lungs. I treated his wound as best I could while he travelled away, into the other place. I did not want to see but our ways are powerful. I was dragged behind him. He had no family around him to call him back. Only me."

"Why has it discovered me? Am I the link between the West and the East? Is this how I am to be used? Have I been granted a vision of the hell that awaits me?"

We stood on a dead land, mired in dark earth. Above us a great void flickered between empty blackness and unrecognised stars. Mist covered everything, sometimes towered into shifting clouds that disguised any horizon. I felt the cold while he, in his turn, sweated out his sickness. Through the mists and far away we could see a sprawling castle whose highest towers rose through the changing sky. It spread like a mountain with foothills of basalt.

"The stone," he whispered, "A peak of the highest tower grows out through the earth there." I did not understand. He turned slowly and pointed with his wounded arm into the far distance, away from the fortress. "And there, in the other place, the Black Tower, rising again through the ground and the snow. A temple. It is here. All around us. It is in the lake, it is in the ground. It is in me."

I could not stand to share his revelations. Suddenly, I saw below us the lake of which he spoke, as if it had just chosen to appear. It was a lake of smoke and, in truth, it lived in its own fashion. The mud beneath us grew slippery. A heavy rain began to fall. I put my hand to my face and found them both covered in blood.

"It falls through the earth," he continued, "Falling and feeding and growing. Our unwitting and unwilling sacrifice to a god no-one can name. All places are one beneath the earth." Then I heard the screams of the dying and I rejoiced. They would draw me home, back to the tent, to the smoke, to the surface of things.

The choking grey smoke of dried twigs turned black and moved without wind. I fought it, rushed at it, lost my senses, opened the tent. The night sky and the voices of death came to me as balm. I realised that I had repeated my failure. I had not the control or the wisdom to divine anything from this.

He sent me away after that. He thanked me for saving him from his wound, which I had healed, but his eyes, now dark and distant, warned me to speak of nothing else. I fear I could not call him back well enough. Part of him was gone.

Will you kill me now?"

The Mongol died quickly and left no trace, as he would have wished. The Englishman's body was flung into a ditch outside of the city walls; an unmarked grave in unhallowed ground. His blood seeped into the earth and sank, finding a home. Though it was not as he would have wished, it was better to die this way.

"And this is proof?" said the student, at last, barely stifling laughter. He placed a hand over the folder in front of them and leaned forward, "You must be joking. This is nothing, just a village inventory and the remnants of a sixteenth century manuscript; Stregoicavar VII/REH. It's meaningless."

"How do you know? What is it to you anyway? Give it to me." He snatched the folder, hugging it to his chest. The student shook his head, smiling. This was no longer quite as amusing as he had first thought. The old man was clearly not right in the head. Time to leave. "Just give me the money," he sighed.

When the awkward transaction was over, the older man glared at the student as he left the tea house. Fool, he thought, you have no conception of what this might mean. History shaped by an unknown belief in ways we have never even thought of? Some unique description of a composite underworld? But the facts, I have the facts here with me now; the missing portions of the Englishman's confession, the copied and recopied versions of the Mongol's words, all hidden or lost and certainly not understood; until now. By me, he thought. Only by me. He opened the folder. Words blurred before his eyes. He passed over papers, flicked back and forth with increasing fear.

There was nothing here, just as the student had predicted. This was wrong. This must be the wrong file. Did I make a mistake? Or have I been duped, set up, tricked? He looked toward the door. The sound of traffic filled the room as the student left.

"Wait!" he shouted, startling the other customers as he stood up suddenly. Running through the shop, he ignored the cries of the waiter. He didn't know the language but it was obvious what was being said. Through the door and into the street, he ran a few yards, shouting at the student's back. As the young man stopped and turned, he ran into him, jostling the two of them out of the flow of pedestrians, to the edge of the pavement. Traffic roared past but he would have been shouting anyway.

"It's not there. It must be the wrong file. What did you do?"

"Get away from me, man, I didn't do anything. Leave me alone."

"You've taken my money. There's nothing in the file that I need. Nothing at all. What is this? Who have you spoken to? Who told you to do this to me?"

"Get away from me," said the student warily, as he stepped back. He was worried now. What if the old fool reported him to the police? It was still theft after all. He had his course to think of. He moved further. The older man reached out to grab his coat. As the student attempted to shake him off, he stepped backward into the road and slipped on the snow. His coat opened in the wind. Then a car struck him, knocking him into the air and five feet down the gutter. The older man was pulled along and lay next to him, staring, frozen, at the dead boy's chest.

Around the accident, traffic squealed and honked. Everyone was shouting. The car that had hit the boy came to an abrupt halt, then another one hit it from behind. The drivers started to emerge, shaken and quiet. After that, the traffic came to a standstill. Over the noise of the commotion, only the few people who had knelt beside the two bodies could hear one of them laughing quietly. The dead body of the student lay in the road, his coat open. The red 'Free Tibet' t-shirt he wore grew darker as blood spilled out and ran to the edge of a drain, pooling slightly before plunging into the abyss. Snow melted in its heat. Black smoke curled lazily from the exhaust just above his unseeing eyes.

Other people helped the old man to sit up but there was nothing they could do to stop him laughing. Beneath the earth, everywhere is one place.

GENERATION

A secret is not something that nobody knows... It is something that nobody tells.

William Watson.

Unseen glass crackled underfoot as the children made their way through the overgrown orchard. Lucas worried about the state of their shoes but they had been so very insistent. Their Mother, he was sure, would not have minded their being here. The Grandmother, however, would almost certainly have never allowed it. But the children were early risers and they had left before the household's breakfast had even been considered. That, he suddenly realised, may not have been such a good idea. He and his wife had always liked the two children. And the children knew how to use that to their advantage. Sighing, he trudged on, trying to keep up.

The spring weather was fine and bright, casting complex shadows over the uneven ground. Up ahead the two little figures of Miles and Maisie raced forward, eager to see the promised ruins at the end of the old gardens. Then, between the trees, black brick fingers, a stunted chimney breast and hidden, dangerous ground, all covered now with bracken and gorse. Lucas had thought the children might like the adventure but they stopped short of the threshold, staring up at the sky. A cloud passed in front of the sun and across the orchard a vast dark wing passed.

It was time to go back.

*

No-one should speak to the servants like that.

Lucas and his wife Ruth, both good people, had been seconds away from leaving before Emily intervened. What was her Mother thinking? An outburst like that was entirely uncalled for. Just because Lucas had taken the children for a long walk on the moor was no excuse for such behaviour. At last Emily felt within her rights to confront her Mother about this persistent unreasonable attitude. The first time in over forty years that the old woman had been persuaded to visit them in what, after all, should surely be called the ancestral home, then within a single day of her arrival she had made both her grandchildren cry and almost lost Emily two faithful servants. It was too much.

The wind was taken out of Emily's confrontational sails when she found that her Mother was preparing to leave as well. With her back to the door she was flinging clothes and books haphazardly into her travelling case on the bed, not caring whether anything would be damaged or even, it appeared, whether the case could be closed over the mess. Without turning around, the seventy five year old woman, still quite obviously vigorous and active, began to berate her daughter with alarming frankness.

"I would never have believed that I had raised you to be such a silly fool. Your father has been gone for a long time but I wish to God he were here now to set you straight on matters. The children could have been hurt out there. I knew I should never, ever have come back here. After all I said you took absolutely no notice whatsoever of me, did not listen once to my recommendations that you and the children should stay in town after Charles was lost. You took no advice from me. Have you ever listened to me, I wonder? Would you even listen to your father?"

"Mother, stop. Please stop doing that. What is so wrong? I have just had to calm Lucas down after the scene you made with him. The children are crying; the house is in uproar. What did they do to make you so...?"

"Do?" Her mother swung round, a handful of scarves flying. Emily was shocked into silence now. Her Mother had been crying. Unheard of. Incredible. "Emily, it was nothing this time. Nothing at all. But... But Miles said they had found a... ruin. A

65

dangerous place. I remember it from when your Father and I lived here. They should not be allowed near it. Don't let them... I don't know how to tell you..." Suddenly she sat down on the bed, an old woman again, swaddled in a pile of dusty dresses and worn-out words.

Emily had never understood this, her Mother's increasingly ridiculous stand against their decision to move back to the house in the country. When Emily's husband Charles had been lost in the War – the family always said lost, never dead, and that merely tradition now - she had taken it upon herself to return to the very place her Mother and Father had left just before she had been born. Emily had been surprised to find that it was still in the family and that, with a few months' work, it had eventually become a beautiful home for her and the two children, hidden in a wooded valley in North Somerset with large grounds and pleasant, considerate neighbours. What could this possibly be about? Perhaps now was the time, finally, to be blunt.

"Why do you hate it here, Mother? Now you are here, after years of us having to traipse all the way to London every time the children want to see Grandma, you can't seriously believe you can leave without giving me some kind of explanation. Please. You'll make yourself ill with this nonsense."

To her surprise her Mother laughed. Not for long though. She took out a handkerchief to wipe her eyes. Still not looking at her daughter directly, she patted the bed, a request to sit down beside her still recognisable from childhood. At last, Emily thought, she's going to tell me a story.

#

Ada Bryant married well and into good stock, as her mother would say. Henry, Lord C. was a fine match for the attractive, if headstrong, young

66

lady. They had been introduced by mutual acquaintances, found each other convivial enough company and, more to the point, the time was right. Ada's mother, the benign tyrant as she had been christened in Henry's sole presence, was adamant that this was the way forward. She also believed but did not say aloud that Henry would be an effective antidote to her daughter's more unusual and less feminine interests.

Science was the thing. The whole mass of nineteenth-century experimentation surrounded Ada like a wild playground. She first took to this recreation because her mother was satisfied that learning would never lead her to waste her life on poetry or novels. In this she was largely correct but the benign tyrant was no prophet. She did not see the potential, the visionary fields of the future, through which Ada began to roam. She read Darwin and Lyell, Davy, Buckland and Edison; even, in her wilder moments, bad, possibly even illegal, translations of Frankenstein and Hroznys. She smuggled in Coleridge in his guise as a commentator on modern progress without even bothering to read his poetry. She even wrote to the Royal Society under an assumed but androgynous name in order to obtain the most up-to-date information. It was obviously time for the institution of marriage to take her in.

"He is handsome," allowed Ada in a whisper.

The tyrant smiled. With that it had begun and ended.

Henry, Lord C. was certainly handsome, if somewhat prone to silence where women were concerned. He enjoyed nothing more than patrolling his estates with a dog or two, encountering his farmer tenants as if by accident and discussing methods of furthering crop yields or rearranging field boundaries. Some said he would have preferred to conduct these conversations at the local inn had he felt he could. But a Lord of the Manor had standards to uphold.

Ada found him to be good man and a good husband. He took her to his family house in North Somerset, on the border of Exmoor, too deep in a valley to spy the sea but large, picturesque and quiet, much like its owner. Ada, finally removed from her mother, breathed easier. Then, after a year of growing accustomed to love, silence and absence, in unpredictable order, she began to read once more.

Somerset was a still a long way from anywhere. She saw no point in accompanying Henry on his trips to other estates round the country and with only two visits a year to her mother in London she was soon casting about the local community for kindred spirits. She felt naively positive about this. Few other women could have brought up the subject of, say, current oceanographic research, at a Porlock dinner party, let alone felt a very pressing need to do so. When, in the course of her fishing for intelligent conversation, the men continued to laugh and the women to frown, she paused to reconsider her situation. Though strange as it may seem, in the end, she need not have begun to worry.

"Will Crosse, this is Lady C."

"Please Jane; you know I don't like to be introduced so formally. Mr Crosse, my name is Ada, and I would be pleased if someone here would just call me Ada for once." Jane, the hostess, retreated, mortified. Will Crosse, who had not had very much to say for himself at dinner, was now standing awkwardly, holding wine in one hand and not drinking enough of it to relax.

"How do you do, Lady Ada,"

"Now that just sounds ridiculous, doesn't it? Please, Ada will be fine. Are you local, Mr. Crosse?"

"Please call me Will, if we are to continue. And yes, I live at Stanhope House on the moor, with my Father." Ada's brow furrowed. Crosse looked

68

suddenly concerned but she laughed and waved her hand.

"I'm sorry. I'm told I look stern when I concentrate. Crosse. I know the name, William Crosse. What does your Father...?"

"Ada, excuse me but my name is not William."

"Oh, I apologise. I did assume..."

"I'm glad you did," Crosse replied, taking a drink, "Most people do. Sadly my name is in fact Wilbur, something I'm not terribly proud of. My Father's name is Victor. I believe you, of all the people here, may actually have heard of him. That is, if your attempts to have a worthwhile conversation over dinner were an indication of your interests."

Will Crosse did not look like a man who had grown up blasted by the heat, wind and cold of Exmoor. Instead he appeared to have spent his entire life underground. Pale skin matched pale, unruly hair. He had been lucky, if that was appropriate, to have been invited to Jane's little dinner party at all. He was, in traditional terms, the last guest, the one to make up the numbers, the one the others felt somewhat sorry for, when they thought of him at all.

After a moment's hesitation Ada said finally, "Victor Crosse, the electrical experimenter. Am I correct?"

"One of a veritable army now, I'm afraid to say. It appears that everyone has a leyden jar in their cellar these days. And a new theory on magnetism or the ether or..."

"Not everyone, Will. Not yet at any rate. And besides, I believe your Father conducts his experiments in a ballroom no less, surrounded, I always imagined, by glass and mirrors, sparks reflecting in the ghosts of pretty dresses..."

"It does have a glass roof, I grant you," Crosse replied, laughing. It was a long time since someone had imagined Victor's laboratory in its former glory. Will had never known it look other than it did today, a blackened maze of metal and acid jars. There were sparks, he knew. Smoke had darkened the glass roof but when the power emerged, there were stars in the room. He was glad Ada had reminded him of the old ballroom. So much of their time now was spent in that stinking cellar.

"Now you look stern. Is there something wrong?"

"No, of course not. I'm sorry. My Father has... moved on in his researches. I was thinking of your talk of the ocean floor."

"Does he look to life now, then? It is not far to go, from the generator to the vessel."

Crosse was amazed. This woman displayed shocking insight. And, he thought, she has sparks in her. And many pretty dresses. He became nervous once more, as he had been all night, until introduced to Ada.

"Would you like to visit? My Father and I, I mean. At Stanhope House?"

"I would be delighted."

*

Henry was away at his Northern estate. Stanhope House lay four miles distant, up on the moor proper; a pleasant hour's ride. It was the middle of summer and everything was alive. Birds, bracken and streams chorused as Ada approached Stanhope House. Will Crosse stood at the foot of the steps and he knew she was bound to be disappointed. His home had not been well looked after for over a quarter of a century. Simple things that servants could have rectified in a day had not been done in years. The windows were filthy. Moss grew between the stones. Inside, he remembered, the dust in some rooms lay as thick as Pompeian ash, or so it seemed on Ada's approach. He forced a smile, wondering what he had to do next.

Ada was indeed disappointed but she soon realised that she had not come here to admire the estate or for social pleasantries. That was her upbringing coming out, the tyrant in her, the woman, she realised, who was happily married to Lord C. She was, in truth, excited to be here. This was her first experience of genuine experimental science, something outside of the books and papers she read. One day, she imagined, all this experimenting will be done in buildings of pristine white, by Societies of Invention, opposing the corruption of black factories, spilling smoke and rubbish into the earth and sky and forcing men and women to toil for too long or have no employment at all. Outside of her reverie, though, the house remained a mess. The Crosses did not keep servants, that much was obvious.

In the garden, beside her as she rode in, a thick electrical cable hung by dirty glass insulators from the unkempt fruit trees. It climbed up onto the roof, disappearing over the top of the house.

"A power source," Will told her, as they entered the gloom of the entrance hall, "Up here on the moors we stand a good chance of picking up lightning from the storms."

"And the Leyden jar for the storage of Nature's power?"

"More than one. And all some of the largest in the world."

The great doors to the old ballroom swung open. The sun through the smoked glass of the roof lent the laboratory an unreal air, the light mottled and strange on the copper coils and brick furnaces. Leyden jars, huge and dangerous, towered over everything, their tops connected to the electric snake that had smashed its way through the roof from the front garden.

"It is magnificent," said Ada, darkening her fingers on the soot that covered almost every piece of equipment. Their conversation consisted of Ada asking a stream of confident questions about the function of everything she could see. Crosse gave her answers to the best of his ability, all the while balancing a nagging worry and a vision of her dancing through the wreckage of a room previously used only for pleasure.

His Father's arrival was heralded by the frightened bleating of a sheep.

"Feeding time. The weather is fine, they eat from my hand, leave the land behind."

Victor Crosse was dragging a small ewe behind him, tied up with rough twine. He looked too old for such strenuous activity but he kept his reluctant partner with him by a combination of grunts and nonsense rhymes. Ada knew him to be in his seventies at least. His eyes were dark and surrounded by dark, as if sleep were something he no longer indulged in. What hair he had left, she noted, was as fair as Will's and as unruly.

"Why are these doors open, Wilbur? Catch your death in a draught of ale, no science can lead us beyond the..."

"Father, we have a guest. This is Lady C. Ada."

Crosse dropped the struggling animal and looked up. He was very surprised.

"Ah. Ah, good evening, your Ladyship; is it evening? I went out but an hour ago. I cannot remember if it was dark then..."

"It is a fine afternoon, Mr Crosse," interrupted Ada, not sure if she was more concerned with the old man's confusion or the state of the poor sheep that was now spinning mournfully on the floor. "I have been admiring your magnificent laboratory."

"Eh? What, this? I haven't been..."

"Father, don't you think we should deal with our livestock first?"

"Oh yes, of course. I'll take it downstairs. It is a rare beast that never sleeps."

"Ada, would you like some refreshment?" offered Will, as his Father struggled off down the corridor. She looked down at her hands and smiled.

"Will your Father be alright with his... partner?" she said jokingly.

"Yes, of course he will. We do it all the time. Forget about that. Follow me now." Surprised at his curt tone, she went after him without further comment.

*

"As you may have judged, I am afraid that my Father is not the man he once was."

Ada, fired by her first encounter, had indulged in a little research. Victor Crosse had indeed been a singular man. One of the last of the great electrical experimenters, he had shown a constant disdain for the 'thunder and lightning brigade' who turned experimentation into a gaudy circus to make society women swoon. He preferred solitude and wrote of nothing but the results of his own repeatable, he insisted, experiments. She finally remembered the circumstances of his fall from popular grace. He had proclaimed, too loudly it had seemed, a discovery of spontaneous generation.

Such a claim would never be popular. The spiritual arm of society, Bishops, vicars, hordes of the outraged devout, closed on him from one side. The temporal arm, his fellow scientists, men he considered to be his equals and some, his friends, rounded on him from the other. Impossibilities had no place in the advancement of learning. No-one took the claim seriously. No-one from the Electrical Society came to view his results. He had moved into an area unworthy of an electrical investigator and,

73

more than that, had thrown himself into the stormy sea of a new biology.

And there he disappeared from public sight.

"It did not affect him too badly, in truth," continued Will, "he has never been one to display his efforts or, as you can see, for socialising. And besides, new avenues soon opened up."

Ada put down her teacup. Will stood at the empty fireplace, staring out of the window at the fruit trees and their artificial burden. He was choosing his words very carefully.

"New avenues?" she prompted.

"Yes. Life has always been a mystery. Not just today. I mean that life, its beginning, its renewal, its continuity, has always been the subject of study. Our science is not the first or the only era in which experiments have been performed."

"You do not believe that the Pyramids house arcane secrets as well, do you?"

"No, no, of course not. I had not meant to imply that... Take your talk of the ocean floor. Our trawlers of the deep have wrenched strange things into the light as a result of our frantic desire to talk to our American cousins with ease. Are you familiar with the work of Ernst Haeckel? Or our own Thomas Huxley?"

"I have heard of Huxley. A disciple of Darwin's?"

"Indeed. Both propose an original form of life, a primordial slime, a first link in the Great Chain of Being. And claim to have found it on the floor of the ocean."

"Better than looking at their wives in such a manner."

Will looked around at Ada but she was not looking at him. Henry, as she had politely put it in an unsent letter once, was not yet interested in having children. Primordial slime indeed. She grew angry at men's inability to see what was in front of them. It seemed that it was more worthwhile, more exciting, to travel as far away from humanity as possible to further knowledge; God on other planets, the source of life on the sea bed while the marriage bed...

"Ada, I am sorry. What have I said to upset you?"

"I apologise. I have not been used to talking about interesting notions with a friendly and understanding companion. In fact, I have not been used to talking of them at all in these last few years. It appears there are concordances within me of which I have been unaware. Please continue."

Now sitting beside her, Will talked of his Father's experiments with *ur-slime*. He did not go into great detail, nor, Ada later realised, could she see any use for the giant ballroom's machinery in his exposition. The laboratory did not look to be in current use, she remembered. Had the electrical snake from the roof broken through the floor as well?

In the months that followed, Ada chose to spend more time at Stanhope House. Will was pleased to have a new friend. Henry did not notice his wife's absences.

*

Inevitably, there was a storm.

October arrived and with it a concentration of bad weather. Nothing could stop Ada visiting Stanhope House at least once a week. She had become more involved in the Crosse household. While staying there she could at least organise some of their haphazard furniture or send a servant over to help with basic housekeeping. Will, initially resistant, gave in slowly, broken down by her new-found gaiety. She had learnt to negotiate the old man's poetic maze, what passed for speech for him in his dotage; but she could not follow all of his digressions. Occasionally Will would have to interrupt their conversation when he felt his Father was becoming confused or, perhaps, when Ada was becoming too interested.

From a windy but bright noon, clouds and rain soon had Ada trapped. She, unconcerned, was excited at the thought of seeing electricity in action. When the first lightning flooded the hallway, she clapped her hands like a child. Victor disappeared. Will stood behind her, indecisive but hypnotized.

"How shall it work? Is it possible to see the power move along the line, up and over and down? No, no, much too fast for that of course. Will it burn at the trees? Shall we have baked apples tomorrow? What shall we do, Will? What shall we do with all this light?

"Ada," he began, taking her clapped hands in his own, "there is more here than light. Darkness is here too, it cannot be avoided."

In his eyes she saw, at last, a decision being made. She did not pull away and he led her by the hand into the ballroom. When the sky cracked white once more she could see that the cable led down, as she had suspected. Some small elements of machinery hummed but nothing indicated that this was the place to be. The lights, other than nature's short, overwhelming bursts, remained extinguished. Will led her to a single doorway in the corner, hidden behind an unused furnace. He turned the handle, opened the door and looked back before descending.

"Not locked," Ada joked, now suddenly nervous, "Nothing too dangerous then?"

"My Father is already down there. He unlocked the door."

"What else?"

"He has unlocked many things in his life."

"No, you misunderstand. What else is down there?"

"Another laboratory, a different kind. I do not know whether you will... appreciate it."

"I will try," said Ada, boldly, "If you will let me see."

Will stepped aside. Ada took ten steps down and, holding the banister, looked over the secret in the cellar.

Smaller by half that the ballroom above, the space stank of too many things to identify. The sea, rot, steam, blood even, wrestled in a soup of sharp, electrified air. In the centre a huge opaque glass tank had been set deep into the floor. The cable from the ballroom was connected to a metal lip around the edge. From this lip a low dome of bars covered the odd vessel.

"A cage?" whispered Ada.

"Yes."

"For what?"

"My brother."

Victor Crosse moved towards the cage, dragging another stunned sheep. There was, Ada noticed, a door in the metal bars that the old man unlocked. He heaved the sheep up into his arms and dropped it into the tank. There was noise as if it had fallen into a thick liquid. He stood back quickly and slammed the door. Another bolt of lightning must have hit the cable because sparks flew as it shut and a noise began, inside the cage.

"My Father called it my brother, his other progeny, when it first... began. He still calls it that though I try to... dissuade him."

Then Ada saw too many things. Something like flesh forced its way up through the bars of the cage, splitting against them like waves on rocks. What passed through remained upright, waving and writhing. At the extremities eyes bloomed, bare, exposed eyes the colour of jewels. Horrified she looked away only to notice signs painted in black upon the floor of the cellar. Words, sigils, circles; the names, she supposed, of demons.

"A monster of science," Ada stared down now at the wooden rail, holding on tightly.

"Science is not enough," stated Will, unsure of what she meant once again.

"No. You, your Father. Was it not enough? Was a scientific monster not enough for you?"

"Ada, it cannot work. All the experimentation we did, all the research, nothing happened. A few unintelligible results with electricity, nothing more. A mat of slimy, green algae that died in a day. He did not wish to put himself through that again. He looked elsewhere. I told you before, we are not the first. Look," he took her arm, "I will show you."

The thing in the tank subsided as quickly as it had appeared. Carefully, Victor Crosse locked the trap door once again. Blood shone on the bars. If his son or Ada had been watching, they would have seen the concern on his face. Something was wrong. Again.

Ada did not wish to descend so soon. Will had to coax her down the final few steps. Even then, she stayed well away from the tank and the markings, almost edging around the wall to avoid being near them. Was this far enough?

"It has a name. But Father and I do not use it. Not a personal name of course. It is... of a type. They are a primal entity, close to our conception of the *ur-slime* in the Great Chain but not of it. It remains something else. Powers of generation, imitation, survival, absorption; every possible protoplasmic development grown – raised - to a macrocosmic level. It experiments with attributes sometimes; an ear, an eye, some implausible limb. And yet it has no sentience we can determine. No point to its existence."

On the wall beside Ada a bookshelf barely supported massive ancient tomes with titles in flaking gold lettering that spoke, in any language but English, of worms, darkness and dead names. How had they taken this path from science into the occult? "That is why he took to calling it my brother," Will continued quietly, "to release us from

78

speaking of demonology when really we should have been measuring, sampling, researching, understanding..."

Ada looked at the tank. There was a noise like small waves. "Did it drive him mad?"

"Yes," Will sighed once more at Ada's painful insights, "The experiments or the creature, I am not sure. Now all we do is feed it. Sometimes we look through the books, hoping for some way to..."

"Destroy it?"

"No, Ada, not that. Communicate, give it real life. Take it from the realm of magic into the realm of science if you like. It is a considerable challenge now."

Ada found herself nearer the tank. Victor Crosse did not move. Instead, in the sanest tone Ada had yet heard from him, he said "You do not have to look at it. There is nothing to grasp." But a glimpse into the liquid seemed inevitable, the only way she could escape the spell. Beneath her gaze a single, half-formed globe tightened like the pupil of an eye. Before she could wonder whether the thing had focused its attention on her, that view disappeared and a mat of cilia grew over the flesh, some questing upward, developing tiny buds. She drew back and returned carefully to the foot of the stairs.

"I'm sorry." said Will.

"I would like some tea," was all Ada could think to say.

*

The storm had not abated. The dark night was filled with rain. Ada could not return home. She was silent for a long time, deciding which question to ask first, which were worth asking, which she dared. Then, abruptly, none of this mattered as Will began to sob uncontrollably. She held him as she wished she had done before this, before knowing his

79

true situation. His head in her lap, she found herself wondering where science could lead. She saw her visions of the pristine clarity of the future obscured by unreadable signs from the past, by mistakes, by iron bars and dead sheep, by the failure of the mind.

She would stay with him. Will and his Father had lost all perspective. They had achieved stupendous things by unorthodox methods but there was a way back. Will's talk of discovering sentience, discovering a future for the thing in the tank, was nonsense, a result of his extended proximity to the madness that had reared the monster in the first place. She felt, too, that even his Father would have agreed with her in some way. He had given up long ago. His interest in the nature of the creature was lost in his derangement. He needed to escape as much as Will.

Yes, she would stay with him.

*

In a very few weeks, Ada was ashamed to discover that she was becoming afraid. Will had been relieved and happy that she had not abandoned him, following his revelation and the onset of a new stage in their relationship but, in time, their differing attitudes toward Victor's other offspring became increasingly evident. At times they argued. During storms, Ada wanted to cut it off from the supply of electricity. Will would not countenance such a disturbance.

"Ridiculous. We have no concept of the interaction between its material and metaphysical form. Such a denial could alter all manner of internal balances."

"You cannot even decide if it is feeding, growing or just existing. Surely any form of

80

experiment must involve changing its habitat or circumstance..."

"I will not allow such drastic measures. Look, here we can go back to its inception. The words of the Arab claim a spontaneous generative nature, even under extreme conditions. It may be that the electrical nature of the cage restricts it in some measure, from precisely the kind of experimentation you advocate."

"I do not understand. Then you do not wish to isolate it because of a concern over a potential increase in its capacity? What could happen? Do these books talk of these things being... unfettered? Let loose?"

Ada was never happy when Will habitually returned to the terrible books he and his father had used to create the creature. She hoped to leave them behind all the more when she sometimes caught Will staring, mumbling phrases from them, back into the worn and yellow pages.

She did not like to work in the basement either, in close proximity to the protean mass. While Will, despite, she felt sure, his own best efforts to the contrary, could not avoid concentrating on the thing's ultimate potential, she came to despise its very nature. She could not understand the continued empty references to it as part of the family, although, in truth, this was only kept up by Will now. His Father had long since ceased talking in his poetic riddles, instead only offering her furtive glances which she chose to interpret as evidence of his own confused concern.

Then Ada's husband returned for an unusually long period: an entire three weeks. She took this opportunity to play the dutiful wife and avoid seeing the Crosses altogether. She cleared her mind of all thoughts of demons and monsters and ran the household with a focus and determination that did not go unnoticed.

"Your energy and application are a credit to you, my dear," Henry told her, over dinner one evening, "I had been under the impression that you spent little time on such drab affairs." With the vast dining table between them, Ada still worried that her husband would notice some small sign of embarrassment.

"On the contrary, a house is a home only when properly run, with all its component parts working together. You and I, the servants, the gardens, the kitchens; all in our place."

"Indeed," Henry replied thoughtfully, choosing to take this as a subtle and, he admitted, not entirely undeserved jibe over his prolonged absences. There could be no more to it than that then.

*

There had been no communications from the Stanhope House for nearly a month now. On the same day that Ada decided to renew her researches, she heard from an altogether unexpected source, news of an altogether unexpected kind. Mr. Victor Crosse, so her maid informed her in surprise, as if the whole town knew before she did, had died a few days past and the funeral was to be held tomorrow.

Could one expect to be invited to a funeral? Should one want to be there? It made no difference in the end. That evening a messenger brought a handwritten note from Wilbur politely requesting her attendance but making no clearer any circumstances or significance. Ada was left in isolation all night, the only one capable of imagining any number of horrendous accidents, and all this despite the protestations of her reliably informed staff that the old man had gone peacefully in his sleep.

The ceremony, held in the draughty church on yet another hill outside town, passed without major incident. Wilbur, on receiving her condolences, would not meet her gaze. Thus she reiterated her intention to visit him as soon as possible rather more loudly than she had intended. He moved away, leaving her confused and miserable. Despite this, when she finally reached Stanhope House, her objectives remained firm.

"Will, you are all alone now. You must do something."

To her surprise, he smiled, and continued his endless circumnavigation of what had once passed for the dining room of Stanhope House. She had long since stopped turning around to follow him. He had been irritatingly uncommunicative since her arrival and she was building to a more forceful interrogation.

"Yes, alone. I know what you are thinking but you cannot continue here alone. It is dangerous," she insisted.

"No. That is not true. With sufficient safeguards in place... there was every reason to believe nothing was changing. There was nothing to indicate..."

"Will, are you going to tell me what happened? I have been imagining all sorts of horrors. The worst... tell me, is it not true?"

"Ada, I am sorry. I was a fool. I thought nothing was wrong, nothing had changed. The creature had not developed, there were no new results. But I was stupid. It was my Father, it was he who was getting old, it was he who had changed, struggling with the cage door, and dragging livestock around the place like some madman... I should have seen it, talked to him, just helped him..." He had stopped pacing. Ada took his hand, their first contact in weeks. Looking directly at her, his voice hardened, "I was at the top of the stairs. He had opened the cage door; I heard it clang down

83

onto the bars when he no longer had the strength to lower it; that was what brought me to the steps. He had nothing with him. No food. He just reached in, stirring the liquid with his arm. He was talking to it, to my brother, but I was too far away to hear.

"What would you expect now? That some monstrous tentacle dragged him into the tank? That he was drowned? That he was crushed by immortal, invisible powers? Nothing like that. He simply fell down. Stopped. When I reached him he was dead. I slammed the cage door closed. Inside I saw a trace of blood sink into the liquid. My Father's hand had been punctured several times. Small holes, nothing that would have caused him pain. Do you know Ada, lately I have been wondering if he had not been conducting his own experiments, in secret, perhaps to this end."

Ada comforted him as best she could but Will was far away, experimenting, alone in his head. She could feel the distance. A trace of his Father's delirium had been left with him. Soon he went back to the abhorred books and Ada left again, saddened and worried. She needed to tell someone, to talk to someone about what was happening but there was no-one in her confidence. Unusually, Henry was at home but he knew of the Crosses as little more than neighbours and, of all people, he could not help her. They had been strange lone investigators, she realised, all of them, not the clear-sighted, reasoning thinkers she had hoped they might become.

For two days and nights she wrestled with her problem. Finally she decided nothing could be done without obtaining, at the very least, Wilbur's consent. Henry watched her from a distance, unwilling to imagine the cause of her distraction.

The day was clear in the morning as she set out. As she rode she knew this was to be the end of things. Whether that involved some kind of exposure, of herself or the creature, she could not say. But there was no continuing with this disastrous arrangement. Wilbur was in no fit state to look after a household of that size, let alone his other, less public, responsibilities.

The wind had picked up by the time she knocked on the door. No-one answered. A light still burned in the front room and hall, probably left from the previous night. She waited patiently but no-one was coming. The door was not locked.

A half-eaten, unappetising meal sat beside an empty decanter of brandy. The glass was missing. She called out, hoping someone would answer, delaying the inevitable.

The glass ceiling of the ballroom darkened almost as soon as she entered. Clouds gathered overhead. Ridiculous, she said to herself, strolling boldly between the machinery to the hidden but unlocked door. From the top of the steps she could see very little. A candle guttered on the workbench set against the side wall, its dying light cut in half by the bookshelves above it. She called out again, but quietly. No reply.

This was the wrong thing to do. She knew it somewhere inside.

But perhaps there had been an accident. Wilbur was merely unconscious. There was nothing to fear.

These were the feelings she had come to loathe. That primal terror of the dark and the unknown; the basement, the storm, the monster. No, it was all too ridiculous, the images redundant in this day and age. The dark seabed has life; it is a source of life and enlightenment. There is the light, she said aloud, down there on the table. Go toward it. Illuminate the darkness. Provide help, if it were needed.

Fortified, she descended the stairs quickly and stalked across the black marks on the floor. She took the flickering candle and lit another beside it. Turning, she saw the cage door was open. More than that, the cage itself was broken and twisted. Upward. Outward. Then a noise like a sheet flapping in the wind. The candle was knocked from her grip. A smothering embrace, a sensation of drowning, all too fast for fear. Then nothing.

*

Ada opened her eyes. She was inexpressibly glad that there were stars above her. Trees moved in the wind. Other noises. Then Wilbur's face over hers, cradling her head. He spoke but she could not hear him. He seemed illuminated by some flickering orange light. The ground was cold. When she attempted to move her arm, everything hurt. She realised her clothes were in ruins. Torn all over, she and they were encrusted with filth. She spat, turning her head to see Stanhope House on fire behind them. She began to shake uncontrollably. Wilbur rocked her at his chest.

"I saved you. I did save you. I did not let it out, it broke out, it moved, oh how it moved... all the creatures of evolution in one conglomerate, changing, adapting. I was entranced. But I saved you. Ada, it backed away. Moved away when I commanded it. It listened, it heard. But I saved you. But the fire began, books and candles, such a foolish mess... It would not leave. Perhaps the electricity..."

Then there was fire on the other side of them as well. Henry and a dozen servants stood by with lamps and torches. There were shouts. Someone knew the location of the well. Six ran off to find it. Over the noise of burning, the sound of shattering glass became quite clear.

"The laboratory..." began Wilbur, as he looked up. Henry took a step forward. Torchlight complimented his expression perfectly.

"My wife has been attacked." A simple statement.

"Yes," whispered Wilbur, "A... animal in the house, a wild... creature was..." But he could not concentrate. He kept looking back at his home, expecting to see some vast shape silhouetted against the flames, taking flight.

"Let her go," ordered Henry. Wilbur lay Ada's head gently down onto his folded coat and stood up. He looked back and forth between Henry's face and the fire.

"She is alive?" Henry asked. Wilbur could only nod. "And the animal?"

Wilbur took a step toward the glowing front door. The roof would fall soon. Shouts came from the darkness of the garden. There was nothing to be done. The place was finished.

"You will not escape," Henry said. Wilbur looked back at him and nodded in agreement. For a single moment he took in Ada's shaking figure, then he walked back into the burning building. Putting down the lamp, Henry knelt beside his wife and began to wipe her face clean. He did not look up until the fiery glow on their bodies was significantly diminished.

#

Her Mother, Ada, Lady C. was in tears. Not deep, soul-cleansing sobs as could have been possible but tears that just emerged from hiding, ran down her cheeks and fell in an endless procession, splashing quietly onto the two hands she held firmly together in her lap. Emily was more moved by this simple crack in her self-possession than by any element of the fantastic story she had just heard. She sat on the bed and took the damp hands in her own. After a time, she felt permission had been given to ask questions.

"How did you discover the end?"

"Oh, your Father told me what had happened. I was in some state of shock for a good while. A month, I believe. After that...During that period we, Henry and I, how do they say, sorted out our differences. We became very close. Very close indeed."

"I understand. What do you think of it now? Of course, I understand now what all the fuss, I'm sorry, what your concerns were. Especially with the children actually going to that place. But the creature, the experiments; it sounds unbelievable Mother. You must know that. You know how it sounds."

"Yes, dear, it does," Ada sighed, "And it is a long time ago and this is the first time I've told anyone. So yes, perhaps unbelievable is how it should remain. I know I would not have told you at all had you not insisted on returning to this place."

"I'm sorry. I would never have put you through this deliberately Mother."

"I know. Sometimes I like to forget everything about it, about who I was, what I knew, who I knew. But then, some good came of it. Can you believe that? You came of it, my darling girl. That bond that Henry and I found, that was you. Always you."

After much making up and clearing of the air, Emily left her Mother to rest. Ada lay back on the pillows, staring at the ceiling. She was an old woman now; secrets were easy to keep. She could not deny that it had been a release to tell her daughter almost everything. Henry had been a good man, a good husband to her for many years. That was certainly true.

But Wilbur Crosse was Emily's true father. She knew that in her secret heart.

*

Emily stopped on her way downstairs to look out of a tall window at her own two children playing in the garden. Fully recovered from the argument of the morning, they were beautiful, a perfectly matched pair. She felt relieved that some secrets were out in the open now. She had always known that something unusual must have happened. It had soon become obvious to her. After the children were born she had tried to uncover the past. Her Mother would be shocked to look at some of the shelves in her own study now. The new sciences of genetics and inheritance had come a long way in a very few years. Further than her Mother. Further even than herself. Great leaps in understanding had been made. And some leaps in generations.

Emily was glad that her Mother had unburdened herself of what she understood of the secret. She felt sure that their relationship would be much improved now. It was enough.

There was a time for telling. And a time for keeping silent.

*

Miles and Maisie were on the edge of the flower bed, watching a rat pick its careful way along the ground against the garden wall. Maisie lay flat on her front, hands before her, feet in the air, counting time with her heartbeat. Miles knelt upright, always interested to see what his sister would get up to next. She was the one who got them into trouble. But it was always fun.

Maisie held her breath. She pointed at the rat. Her index finger grew longer, its tip sharper than a dagger. Three feet away the rat was skewered with only time to let out a short squeak. Miles grinned.

"Ow," his sister muttered. She had hit the wall behind the rat. Flexing the impossible finger, she flicked the corpse into the air, towards Miles. He caught it in his mouth, suddenly grotesquely expanded, swallowing it whole, trying not to giggle.

Maisie rolled onto her back, rubbing the finger as it grew smaller again.

"Mummy said we're not supposed to play when we've got visitors," whispered Miles, when he could speak again.

"I know that," replied his sister, "But no-one saw, did they?"

THE TIP OF THE ICEBERG

It may surprise you to learn that I am now perfectly content to die on this ice at the bottom of the world. My indifference would certainly have surprised my previous compatriots. William, I am sure, would have been the first to express a wish to survive and tell our tale in person. But he was not allowed the chance, while I am to pass away cold and alone. I shall not grow old bones.

I believed I was the first to sign up for our momentous journey and thus, in some small way, stood at the forefront of what my father insisted on calling "a voyage in the grand tradition of the ship of fools". I was also the youngest, and by far the least famous and the least qualified, to join a scientific expedition into the Southern Oceans. But I was ambitious; more, I was a strutting intellectual, as confident of my own genius as I was of the rightness of our course.

"I have no idea what you are talking about," William said to me, within a week of our ship, the *Caliban*, leaving port. "You are, sir, extravagantly well read in the most fashionable theories I have ever had the pleasure to encounter. But you are not, my lad, on a par with my friends and I. It matters not, however, as we are all glad to have your company and your contribution to our efforts. I have no doubt that the Royal Society will welcome you back with open arms when we are successful." He paused, and smiled. "But I get ahead of myself. I shall introduce you to the others and we shall let you in on our little secret because, as you can see only too well by now, we are sufficiently trapped by the elements to ensure our project and our findings remain within these bulkheads."

He was right of course. We were heading south from the Cape into unknown waters. Captain Cook had passed this way and Weddell had mapped some airy possibilities but, truth be told, soon enough there would be no-one else within a thousand miles, except such whalers as braved the

94

eternal cold. We too were on a whaling ship, such as it was, named appropriately for the wizard's pet monster. It had been recast, at considerable expense, as an exploratory vessel, and was now capable of pandering to needs of a more scientific nature. Our Captain, Adam Seaborn (an unlikely name, perhaps concealing an unsavoury past, I felt), told us that he was enormously fond of his ship and that, monstrous though she was in both looks and title, she had the strength of a beast and would survive the most brutal travails.

So it was that, fortified with port and brandy, I was officially introduced to Robert Amos Bennett, geologist, evangelist and tee-totaller, and to Willis George Emerson, gentleman, experimenter, atheist and drunkard. Somewhere between the two, in both consumption and conception, was William Bradshaw. He had been a friend of my father's until some trifling falling out had separated them for some years. I, for my part, had always enjoyed Bradshaw's company and kept in touch, especially when my education began to lead me towards his peers. William, with his secure family income and influential friends, had helped me through Oxford and suggested my name to the panel that had put together this private expedition. So, in a way, he is the one I have to thank for my present state. Damn his eyes.

"You want to be a botanist, I hear" boomed Emerson, not deigning to avert his eyes from the brandy in his glass in order to look at me.

"Yes, sir. I have studied Lamarck in detail and I have had the pleasure of a personal interview with a certain Mr Darwin on his return from a most fascinating voyage. I believe I can see great things emerging in this field and would like to make my mark there."

"I don't hold with it," remarked Bennett, "I consider it a trespass upon the dominion of religion." He sat upright at the table, swaddled in a greatcoat and furs and apparently unaffected by any movement of the ship. This, before it had even turned cold. He suffered well and gladly and I found him a very strange man. I was not, however, cowed by his objection.

"You are a geologist, are you not? Why does one discipline serve the Lord and another displease him? Are we not all God's work?"

"His work is done. It is there for us to see and explore. These theories of life are not the same as a history of the rock we live on. Nature, his Will, does not continually tinker with his living creations. Processes, developments, are an illusion. The Great Chain of Being is thoroughly in place and is precisely that: a chain with which we are bound. We shall prove it. There are ways."

I had thought to take the argument further but William stepped between us.

"Our little secret, remember? Don't you want to know what we are all doing here, youngster?"

"I had thought we were on a voyage of discovery," I replied, looking pointedly at Bennett, "Was I incorrect?"

"Oh, not at all, lad," said Emerson, "We are on the greatest journey of all time, mark my words. We shall toast the heavens, or possibly the depths, if we are right."

"If Symmes is right," corrected William. "Do you know him, lad? John Cleeve Symmes of Ohio, North America?"

"I fear I have not had the pleasure."

"A great man," William continued. "A visionary," To add drama to this suddenly grand tone, he took a step back and gave a short speech which, as I soon grasped, all three men already knew well.

" 'I declare the earth is hollow and habitable within; containing a number of solid concentric spheres, one within the other, and that it is open at the poles twelve or sixteen degrees. I pledge my life in support of this truth, and am ready to explore the hollow, if the world will support and aid me in the undertaking'".

He declaimed this in such reverent tones that the others looked up at him as if he might have been quoting scripture. I felt a distinct sinking feeling in my stomach, separate from the rise and fall of the ship. Emerson, enlivened now that our project was at last out in the open, stood with his brandy to complete the picture.

"Yes, that was his proclamation in 1818 to the world. Of course he was ignored. He sent his letter to all and sundry, claiming Sir Humphrey Davy and Von Humboldt as protectors. He wanted to pursue an expedition to the North Pole there and then. Again, it came to nothing. But we and our backers, of whom you may have heard but I cannot name names, looked into this with interest. And, finally, we have set upon this course of action. The *Caliban* shall sail to the edge of the world, the hole in the pole, to prove his theories and to make our names as legends..."

I drank no more that night. I had discovered much that disagreed with me and would not have added to my sickness.

The next morning I stood alone on deck. The grey sea and rolling cloud could not distract me from my dismay. I confess that my reputation was the uppermost thought in my mind. The reputation I had not even the chance to gain before it would be dashed by their nonsense. I feared that my father was right. I sailed on a ship of fools, amongst them, his old friend.

Captain Seaborn shouted orders over the winds, keeping his sailors in good order and preparing for inevitable storms. They worked tirelessly, it would seem, knowing their trade inside out. Seeing me slumped over the railings, the Captain tipped his hat in my direction. I acknowledged him with a wave of the hand, feeling better, suddenly, for his attention. Perhaps I should still be able to make something of this. Of course I should. I had my work to do, just as every man here did. I was still in a unique and enviable position, regardless of my companion's theories. If I had a reputation to make, then I would make it in opposition to such ridiculous notions, if need be. I felt a blast of cold wind take the ship in a new direction and, newly fortified by such minor omens, resolved not to allow the others to distract me from my researches.

This is not to say that, after that first strengthening morning, all conflict was at an end. On the contrary, I spent many hours in futile argument with Emerson and Bennett while William attempted in vain to keep us on an even keel. I pointed to any number of perfectly adequate theories that would have proved my points to the most ignorant savage but it was to no avail. Emerson opposed me with every technical detail at his disposal and, as a scientist, he could not be faulted in his handling of rhetoric, tying me up in knots whenever I took him to task on the nature, age and construction of the planet. I found I had no issue with him on many subjects. It was only the conjectures of a hollow earth that sustained a rift between us.

Bennett, on the other hand, was consistently and coldly angry during our frequent debates. He accused me of having limitations in both learning and imagination. I took offence that a man so bound by religious dogma could accuse a fellow scientist of having a limited imagination. William was duty bound to step in at this juncture. He managed to silence Bennett's riposte. I feel sure the man was about tell me that I was not considered a 'fellow' anything.

I did talk to William about my predicament. I told him that I was disappointed that he had kept such an extraordinary interest from me until after our departure. To his credit, he immediately recognised my position and apologised as best he could.

"But all the same, don't you feel it? This is the opportunity of a lifetime. To change our view of the world forever. To travel beyond limits. In all honesty, my young friend, deep down I have my own doubts about our hypotheses but it will not keep me from trying. There is something here, I swear it."

He was right of course. At the time I could not deny it as it appealed to my new and personal sense of purpose. Now I know he was right and it leaves me cold. Very cold indeed.

We saw our first iceberg on a fine day. A line of white on the horizon became a block, then an island, then a vast blue white monument. It silenced us all. No matter what our beliefs, all four of us stared at the thing as it slid past. The whalers and the Captain, intent on not hitting the huge block, carried on their essential tasks as ever. They had seen them before.

As it receded, we all began to talk at once. I marvelled at the colours, looking forward to mobile colonies of penguins and seals. Bennett wondered aloud how we could obtain samples. Emerson described the layering of the ice, the colours, the possibility of sediments, the origins. William simply said, innocently, "I wonder how old it is?"

I cannot dwell on the following weeks. Excitement gave way to numbing, eternal cold. Soon enough the sea began to freeze. Captain Seaborn had urgent and private meetings with William. I was told we had gone further south than any previous explorer. Moving through a never-ending daylight, we pushed on. Icebergs now became our constant companions and, instead of working, the crew took to grumbling and worrying. Arguments broke out, more significant and heated than our precious academic rivalries. The *Caliban,* that big and ugly monster, pressed on, cracking the sea before it like an axe. As I hung down over the bow, to watch the then thin ice break up before us, I slowly became aware that the landscape was taking us over. The heavy weight of the ship, so solid and imponderable out there on the calm ocean, was being overwhelmed by the cold and its physical avatar, the unending ice.

In the Southern Ocean we had endured but one single storm, though it had lasted a good three days. A miracle, Captain Seaborn had declared. An omen, said Bennett, with a challenge to me in his eyes. Quite enough, was all I could manage to contribute. Since then, a very reasonable wind had kept us on course.

Then it was gone.

We drifted this way and that, the ice pushing us hither and thither. After our evening meal, or what passed for an evening and a meal at that latitude, I found I had drunk a little too much.

"Where is it then?"

"I beg your pardon?"

"Where is it? The hole? Six thousand miles across, you told me only last week. Yes, Emerson, I understand, before you jump in. We may not notice the change. The edges will be vast. Soon enough we will be sailing upside down! Inside the earth! Without a care in the world presumably. Where it is warm. With an internal sun. Or even two. Sirs, I do not care for this new definition of heat."

Whatever the truth behind my outburst, I had gone too far. Bennett rose without a word and left the room to retire to his cabin. The cold as he left also announced the arrival of the Captain. He had the look of single-minded intent about him. I wished more than ever that I had not drunk so much.

"Mr Bradshaw," he always addressed William in the first instance, considering him, rightly or wrongly, the leader of our merry band, "we must turn back if and when we can. In all honesty, the crew and I fear for the safety of the ship and our lives. We have seen no land and no change in the weather. We cannot go forward like this. In fact we cannot go forward at all. We must push off with staves, crack the ice and find open water, in readiness for a wind, which, God willing, will soon come. I'm sorry; Sir, but I see no other course of action."

It was the first time that the full content of William's conversations with the Captain had been placed openly before us, though we could all have guessed had we wished to do so.

"Damn it," shouted Emerson, slamming his glass down, "I put all my money into this. I'll not be turned around by the cold."

"Robert, you do not feel it with brandies to insulate you. What will you do when they run out? And you cannot deny, that will be very soon." It appeared that William had had enough of playing the arbiter. Emerson drained his glass. William turned to the Captain. "Do as you see fit, Captain Seaborn. We have achieved a great many things on this voyage. We already have a wealth of information to impart, both scientifically and geographically. It would be a shame if that was lost as a result of...an excess of zeal on our parts." The Captain barely had time to express his thanks before he was up the stairs, shouting at the crew to break out the something or others and get us out of this damned ice.

Draining the last port from the ships decanter, Emerson rose unsteadily from his chair and addressed his parting remarks to me. "I hope you're satisfied now, lad. Tell'em what you like. Waste of time and money. Fools. Damn them all." In my equally befuddled and somewhat embarrassed state, I could not establish precisely to whom he was referring and so let him leave without comment. The cold as the door opened once again did at least serve to sober me somewhat.

"I'm sorry, William."

"Don't concern yourself. He will be over it in the morning."

"No, I mean about the expedition, about the...venture. About the new land in the earth."

"Ah, that," he sighed quietly, looking deep into the last glass of port. "Yes, it would be good to feel the heat of another sun, to sail under an alien sky. Just the once."

I felt, but did not mention, that we were doing just that.

Outside the crew set to work with a ferocity born of fear. I have to admit that our tiny band of intellectuals, cocooned in abstract work and even more abstract beliefs, realised little of the fatal potential in our situation. All of us, myself included, simply left the sailing to the sailors, retreating to our notebooks and categorising, our greatest irritation, the frozen ink. I tried to comfort myself with the mass of observations I had made. Naturally I had a certain advantage over the others. As yet, my hopes and dreams of success and recognition remained not entirely fanciful. As such, I was pleased when I felt the ship move once more.

As I made my way on to the deck, bundled up as best I could be against a light wind that, I hoped, heralded our retreat from the ice, I saw, for the first time, the Iceberg. The weak, low sun shone behind it, darkening some areas, glinting off others. It seemed unusual in shape, though I doubt I was an expert on these things. It listed in the water, and the surface, relatively flat but with a thick spire pulling one side down and exposing new blue ice at its side, appeared to be a confused mass of broken snow. At the railing, I saw the crew hastening back on board. Around us the cracked ice slid over itself, creaking and splashing. The iceberg was drawing nearer all the time. I could see flashes of black open water in its path.

"I fear we may have got ourselves a travelling companion. This wind's blowing it in our direction but we can't move out," muttered Captain Seaborn, appearing beside me.

"How big would you say?"

"Bigger than it looks. They always are up close,"

Amidst the increasingly shrill shouts and orders, the iceberg approached the side of the ship. In a few hours, both wind and temperature dropped. We became stuck fast again with the berg a few dozen feet away. The spire loomed above us, so close the sailors took to throwing ice at it until the Captain gave them better things to do. I walked the length of the ship to get a look at the blue ice near the base. William joined me, shivering with cold.

"I fear Emerson is coming down with some degree of frostbite. I have no idea what Bennett may be suffering. How are you, lad?"

"I am fine for the moment. Rather overwhelmed by this mountain. William, can you see that, down there by the ice line?"

In the transparency shapes emerged. Dark colours hid in the ice. We looked closely. Clarity eluded us, but there was something.

"Should we look further?" I wondered. William went to talk to the Captain. I considered informing the others but decided to let William make the decisions. I did not wish to make myself more unpopular than I had already become. Eventually William returned with worrying news.

"We can do as we wish, he says. I am afraid he is not in the best of moods, with us, his employers, in particular. His crew will be out on the ice using ice saws to cut us free, he hopes. That thing will only hinder our escape. This has become altogether too dangerous a venture for him."

"But we should go regardless," I pressed. "Bennett will want to study this thing at close quarters at least."

The three of us stood on the ice before a clear blue wall. Emerson, refusing to join us, was finishing what he claimed was his last and best bottle of wine. I believe he never saw our Pandora's Box.

"What is that?" William said. Three men of science, at the bottom of the world, rendered almost speechless.

"I cannot see," said Bennett, stepping closer, and brushing damp and ice from the berg's side. We gazed through his makeshift portal at another world.

"Titans," I suggested, my imaginings spoken aloud.

Nearest the surface, some form of huge plant leant at an impossible angle toward us. Tendrils from it passed though the ice, further confusing any solid outline. A five-lobed head emerged from a barrel-shaped body. Similar figures, two, perhaps three, were behind it, twisted and rent in a way that brought to mind some fearsome struggle. For behind them all, and the source of the darker colour I had spied from the boat, was a vast mass of shapeless matter, seeping between the pieces, like tentacles, hands ripping the bodies asunder. This mass descended far into the berg, beyond our limited, confused vision. Some ancient avalanche had caught these creatures in the midst of their titanic battle. Centuries of gradual movement had twisted their bodies into these ghastly shapes. Surely that must be the explanation.

But they were like nothing I had ever seen. The closest approximations to their general structure were the creatures seen through a microscope but here they were, larger than life. And this possibility went no way toward explaining the preposterous nature of the dark mass behind them. As I peered still further, I thought I could make out other organs erupting from the darkness. Pseudopods, mouths, even teeth, vestigial eyes glared back at me. I stepped away. None of this was clear. The ice was too deep for any certainty. I remembered William's simple question: how old?

Before I could formulate any useful enquiry, Bennett stomped quickly back to the ship, passing through the men sawing at the ice with singular purpose.

William repeated himself, quietly, as if he asked the question of God.

"What is that?"

I returned to the ship, stepping more carefully than Bennett on that thin ice, unnerved, but keen to get my sketch and note books. Emerson snored fitfully in the cabin. In my haste I could not find sufficient paper and went to ask Bennett for assistance. Excitement overcame my dislike of the man. I found him crouched over a huge volume that I had never seen before. All in all, there were many things I had never seen before, the most surprising of which were his tears.

"Proof, you wanted," he said to me before I could open my mouth. "Proof of other worlds. Well, I am sorry to say that I have had it here all the time." There was an edge of hysteria in his voice which kept me silent. "I was led here by this, this passage; I felt, I believed in my innocence, that the South Pole was "where the Spheres meet." I took this as a... a literal metaphor so to speak, a ray of light in this otherwise repulsive work of a damnably insane foreigner. A precursor of Symmes, the origin of legends. But now, oh now there are other things that come out of the pages. Abominable tales of creatures like those remains out there. What can this tell us now, eh? What does this prove? If this blasphemous compilation of hoary myths can lead me here and show me this, of what else is the Lord capable? Look for yourself, damn you! See where science can lead!"

I saw little of science in my swift perusal of the ancient tome. I saw alien sorcery, fantastic names, Kadath, Yog-Sothoth and ritualistic cadences in apocalyptic Biblical style; "Their hand is at your throat, yet ye see them not". How anyone could lend credence to such nonsense was beyond me. But it had affected Bennett so strongly. And even I could see, perhaps, some familiarity in singular descriptions of certain ancient demons. And here we were, in an undeniable "ice desert of the South" as the book mentioned. My first thoughts, though, and I said as much to the staring Bennett, were of Lamarck and his theories of the development of organs in living creatures. I said this to calm his nerves but instead he laughed at me, causing frozen tears to fall to the floor.

I suppose it was this encounter that saved me, if that is an apt description of my current state. Recovering my books and writing utensils, I set out in a daze, over the side of our poor frozen ship, past the increasingly frantic crew and out onto the endless plain of ice. Too many thoughts crowded my mind. The limitless glowing horizon was not sufficient distraction from the enormity of my thoughts. I stumbled and fell before finally turning to survey the activity behind me. Automatically I took up a pencil and sketched the scene.

The possibility that we were the agents of our own destruction is the cause of much absorbing debate between myself and the seals hereabouts. I could see William, still intent on the side of the berg. He was approached, warned presumably, to step away, by the Captain. The crew, with their sawing and hacking, appeared to be making little impact on the ice plain that encased the ship and, from this small distance, I could hear an ominous increase in the creak and strain of our natural prison.

A resounding crack echoed over the ice. Dark water appeared between the berg and the ship. With awful clarity I saw both William and Captain Seaborn drawn under the ice, hands slipping on the blue wall. The ice pinnacle rose above the ship. It seemed for all the world that the thing was intent on attacking the vessel. The crew scattered, jumping for their lives over disintegrating masses of unstable ice. Few were successful in maintaining themselves for more than a minute. I believe I saw Bennett emerge onto the deck. He was looking upward at the aggressor, holding his arms aloft as if he welcomed the end.

The Iceberg turned over in the water. The pinnacle, now some giant spike of an ice-axe, smashed through the decking. Spars and timbers splintered beneath its weight. Debris was flung out by the impact, scattered beyond even my position. I barely noticed the black lightning forks of water approaching me. The tall, ice encrusted masts fell together, showering the scene in glinting ice crystals. I thought of Emerson, drunk and drowned.

A pattern emerges. This was not the worst of it. Black silhouettes of the crew, either scrambling on ice rafts or bobbing about in that lethal water, began to scream. Why not, I thought, numbly. Why not? Then I saw the underside of the Iceberg, newly exposed to the pale sun.

There was more of the dark creature there. As water ran away over the smooth curves, it became apparent that the berg's underside was far larger than we had imagined. Whether this inversion is a common occurrence, or even, I hesitate to add, a natural phenomenon, I will never be in a position to know. The organic mass took up fully two thirds of the exposed ice which nestled firmly against the listing, drowning *Caliban*. In some places chunks had been broken away by the violent upheaval, exposing what I can only think of as naked flesh.

My encounter with Bennett and his outrageous tome had already left me irreparably confused. My indistinct vision of the prodigious creature in the ice and it's ridiculous organs, the unavoidable questions of age and provenance, all combined to overwhelm any semblance of scientific detachment. How old? How can such things come into being? How can such a protean mass develop such recognisable and yet arbitrary limbs? Over how many epochs? And yet, in one organism? Retaining all functions over that time? What of the smaller, plant creatures, torn apart so long ago? By the ice? By their pursuer? What manner of life had existed here? Any theories I ever knew, any foundation I had ever believed in, was inexorably crushed, drowned and frozen.

It was still alive.

The exposed flesh seeped like a viscous fluid over the surface of the berg then reared up in anomalous shapes, as if searching for the correct form, adapting before my very eyes to an environment so hostile to the screaming men left alive. When I saw this I took an involuntary step forward. It was not the last vestiges of scientific wonder that drew me. Instead it was more some primeval urge to throw myself into the thing's questing embrace, to make the questions cease once and for all. I felt it call inside my head. More debris clattered and splashed around me as the thing twisted about. It remained trapped in the ice while the wreckage of the *Caliban*, appearing to grow stronger in her death throes, bore down on it, masts and sails snapped and unravelled. It touched men and they fell beneath its embrace. Others chose death by water. As I said, I could hear screaming but by the end there was only mine and that of the creature, indistinguishable in my head.

The iceberg, the creature and the wreck of the *Caliban* formed an unstable alliance. First one and then another righted itself, all, to my view, showing a distinct will to survive. Soon enough though, they all lost the fight and sank, bubbling, beneath the cold sea. As they disappeared the ice floes moved to cover the exposed wound and I felt a shudder when the patch of ice on which I stood became detached. I fell, scattering paper. Not daring to move as I drifted, I saw bodies, ice-rimed, floating in the water, surrounded by splinters of wood. There was no more noise, except the odd bump of ice against ice. I stared at the white sky and white ground as the sea froze around me once again. Only one thing attracted my attention, a tiny object, ejected toward me during the battle and lying only a few feet away. When I felt sufficiently safe to move, I crawled toward it.

My fingers are blackened beneath these gloves. My feet are no longer my own. Why, in this world of whiteness, does flesh turn to the reverse? The seals have joined me, remaining at a distance and laughing at my end. The world is not as I believed it to be and I am no longer sure we can hope for a better one to come. The last thing I found, washed up from the archaic depths, was an ornament. A fashioned, deliberate, metallic decoration, a small model of one of the plant creatures, wrenched from the unthinkable past for a few moments only to be lost again as surely as before. Why was this my final revelation? Perhaps it was merely to prove to me, before I died, that advanced civilisations of monstrosities, not animals, not plants, had lived and flourished long before Man, that the universe is upside down, and that my world is, as predicted, hollow.

WHAT DANFORTH SAW

(OR 'A FINAL PLUNGE')

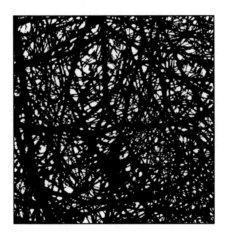

We are surely doomed to hover continually upon the brink of eternity, without taking a final plunge into the abyss.

Edgar Allan Poe,
MS Found in a Bottle.

The cup brought it all back to him again. He could never say precisely what it was that forced him to throw the innocuous china against the shuttered window and begin to scream for the third time that week but it drew the nurse to his bedside in a hurry. He did not fight. He never does. Even so, it is obviously unnerving to have your patient sat bolt upright, with their eyes screwed so painfully shut it hurts even to look at them, and screaming. The nurse can only call for the Doctor, who calls for medication once again. When it takes effect, finally, too late to avoid setting all the other patients off on their own journey down into darkness, he calls for Dyer. He needs to tell him again, to hear himself say it, get it out so he can pretend it wasn't real. At least he was only screaming incoherently this time, not saying that word over and over. Perhaps he is getting better.

In 1930 an expedition from Miskatonic University, Arkham, Mass. left Boston Harbour for the Antarctic. Its main aim was scientific, specifically to test, under Polar conditions, the efficacy of a new drilling rig in recovering geological samples. Secondarily, it was the first such expedition to use aeroplanes as a primary mode of transport, thus incorporating, of necessity, mapping and exploratory innovations as well. Early successes in all these fields were overshadowed by the time of the expeditions return. As with so many things, what started well, ended badly.

By early 1931 the expedition was in disarray, not for any of the reasons that normally afflict adventurers in that "awful place" but due to other, less tangible forces.

Following the discovery of (at the very least) a previously undiscovered wall of mountains (lat.

112

76° 15', long 113° 10'), the deaths of several members of the party and the subsequent breakdown of a student named Danforth, the surviving party retreated from the continent.

> Under a cryptic sky, the landscape itself becomes a vast cryptogram which, once it is unravelled, reveals to man his insignificance in the cosmic scheme of things.

-Angela Carter, 1978

Further information is contained in a manuscript by the Geology Professor of the expedition, William Dyer (made accessible to the public by H.P. Lovecraft). The latter and more debatable section of the Dyer manuscript tells of the remarkable discovery of an ancient, ice-covered city of non-human origin and of its subsequent partial exploration by Dyer and Danforth. Their story lays out a complete prehistory of a non-human earth populated by intelligent but wholly alien beings; the Old Ones. These beings created all life on earth and slave 'animals' called shoggoths. Even these masters and monsters shunned a further immense range of mountains as containing an evil too great for even their tastes.

Dyer and the student Danforth were the only two men to fly over the new range of mountains and bring back this information. It was at a point during their return flight that Danforth lost his reason on making the Biblical (or, classically, Orphean) mistake of looking back[1]. Dyer is at pains to point

---

[1] In fact this was the second time Danforth had looked back and regretted it. The first is when both Dyer and Danforth see what is chasing them through the tunnels of the ancient city. On their return flight Danforth, when his condition forces Dyer to take over the controls of the plane, has not apparently learnt from his previous shock.

out that Danforth only looked back for a very short time: "Danforth did not hint any of these specific horrors till after his memory had had a chance to draw on his bygone reading. He could never have seen so much in one instantaneous glance." So it is only later, when Danforth has been hospitalised after his breakdown that, in his weakened state, he whispers "disjointed and irresponsible" things about his final vision to his only possible confidante, Dyer. It should be noted that his visions, if real, may only have been reflections in the cloud formations above further, higher mountains. The manuscript continually makes reference to unusual reflections in the sky and the inability to distinguish between actual landscape and distorted images. It is also true that Danforth specifically claims "as soon as he gets a grip on himself" that all he saw was a mirage, at most a confused, badly remembered reflection in the sky of "what lay back of those other violet westward mountains". But it is obvious from his condition that this is not the whole story.

Danforth himself was one of seven graduate students from the University on the expedition. Significantly, he was "a great reader of bizarre material, and talked a good deal of Poe". This is a crucial admission when considering his later statements. On his return he attempts to contain his problems by referring back to his earlier outré reading as, at least partially, a source and inspiration. This prop, this excuse, cannot contain his final decline. His reading both supports and explains his visions. His fiction drifts too easily into fact.

Dyer's report of what Danforth saw consists of thirteen items and "other bizarre conceptions", beginning with *the black pit* and ending on *the original, the eternal, the undying*. These are what the stricken student sublimated from a single moment of crisis, previous hours of extreme stress and a lifetime of strange and obscure reading. I have tried

to   expose   some   possible   "disjointed   and
irresponsible" sources below.

> *William Dyer sits by Danforth's bed. He
> has an urge to hold the young man's
> hand but is confused. Danforth is just a
> student, Dyer, a tenured Professor. It
> would not do. And yet they have seen
> more together than anyone should ever
> see. They know, they believe, more than
> anyone on earth is capable of
> understanding. Dyer is on extended leave
> after the expedition. He looks around at
> the walls of the ward, sees other humans
> existing in other beds, and sees the stain
> on the shutter where Danforth's drink
> made its mark. The young man is curled
> up now, hands out in front of him, eyes
> still closed, calmed on the outside by
> drugs. In the end Dyer knows this all
> means nothing, reaches out for the hands
> on the bed. Danforth begins to speak.
> Dyer leans closer, trying, against his will,
> to listen.*

The Black Pit

> For (the atheistic pessimist) the *ultima
> Thule* is earth and matter, and he
> sees, beyond the *prima materia,* only
> an ugly void, an empty nothingness.

> H.P. Blavatsky
> *The Origin of Evil,* 1917

A common, if gothic, beginning.

Helena Petrovna Blavatsky, founder of the Theosophical movement (Maroney, 2000 and Washington, 1993) and something of a charlatan, refers to the South Pole as "the *pit*, cosmically and terrestrially – whence breathe the hot passions blown into hurricanes by the cosmic Elementals, whose abode it is." (Blavatsky, 1888, pg274) Her vision, quoted above, of the "ugly void" could be considered the starting point for the 'cosmic horror' that Danforth and Dyer experience. Her 'atheistic pessimists', easily recognisable in the materialist scientists on the Miskatonic Expedition, are not, in the end, faced with nothing at all but with a distinctly alien, anti-human alternative. The void is not actually empty; what is there simply has nothing to do with us, even though it contains our origins. At best it is accidentally inimical.

Given the Antarctic setting (the *ultima Thule* of Blavatsky and others despite its original location north of the British Isles), this could be read as the beginnings of an alternative, somewhat modernised version of Edgar Allan Poe's vision of a huge whirlpool of water from *The Narrative of Arthur Gordon Pym*, perhaps the most famous "bizarre" memoir concerning the Southern Polar region. The *pit*, its position and the limited descriptions given by Danforth also call to mind certain Hollow Earth theories of the previous century.

That the earth is hollow and access to the interior allowed by holes at both poles is an idea with a surprisingly tenacious grip on the human mind. The Jesuit polymath Athanasius Kircher first wrote of such possibilities in his *Mundus Subterraneus* (1665). Since then the idea, with both great and subtle variations, has enjoyed reasonably constant attention from autodidacts, dilettantes, mystics and Nazis. Even as far back as Kircher though, the initial prompting was the limits of exploration, being forced to only imagine what might be beyond the forbidding and then impassable seas of ice. As Joscelyn Godwin says (in the definitive study *Arktos: the Polar Myth in Science, Symbolism and Nazi Survival)* "This deficiency of practical experience could, however, be made up by logical reasoning in combination with tradition". And so it has been, many times over.

Perhaps the most significant and one of the most widespread theories was that of John Cleeve Symmes who, on April 10th 1818, publicly declared that "the earth is hollow and habitable within; containing a number of solid concentric spheres, one within the other, and that it is open at the poles twelve or sixteen degrees." Symmes maintained this belief until the end of his life (Collins, 2001). This particular theory directly influenced Poe's Pym narrative, which, in turn, influenced Danforth. There are significant echoes of Symmes in Danforth's later utterances, as I hope to show.

There has always been debate about the position and movement of both the South Pole and any hypothetical entrances found on or near it. The precise location of Danforth's vision then, even after Richard Byrd's flight over the Pole in 1929, is not necessarily problematic. What matters more is the place of the Hole in the mind. From Kircher to Danforth, a particular psychic space has opened up that cries out for definition. The Iron Mountains, the Mountains of Madness, the island of Tsalal, even the flickering, reflected archipelago of Megapatagonia all exhibit the liminal, borderland caprices of an existence between fiction and reality. They are part of the Antarctic rabbit hole into which Danforth has fallen.

Antarctic tales seem to have a peculiar penchant for *lacunae* or holes.

In this respect, Danforth's visions perform, for the Dyer narrative, a similar function to the lost chapters mentioned in the appended note to Poe's *Narrative of Arthur Gordon Pym*: "The loss of two or three final chapters...is the more deeply to be

117

regretted, as, it cannot be doubted, they contained matter relative to the Pole itself, or at least to regions in its very near proximity..." The information of the greatest significance, of the most danger, the "final plunge", is somehow consistently lost or postponed.

Jules Verne's sequel to Poe, *Le Sphinx de Glace*, while resolving certain unanswered questions from the original in a science fiction style true to the author's fame, singularly fails to engage a larger issue and, in doing so, almost accidentally continues the air of eternal mystery. The final discovery of Pym's body and the "colossal magnet" that drew him to his death overshadows the obvious question: why is there a huge block of ice in the recognisable, "mythological" shape of a Sphinx near the South Pole? Verne suggests that this is the "shrouded human figure" that Pym sees at the very end, indicating an even more specific, less incidental, shape. What form better suggests ancient mystery? This is the kind of fear and inscrutable wonder that Poe, Pym, Danforth and Dyer encounter; Verne simply ignores it[2].

The Carven Rim

If the majority of what Danforth sees is contained in or around *the black pit* with *the carven rim*, this implies, as it should, a further development of the teleological horror described in the narrative proper. Taken literally, the potential for imaginings is immense; who or what carved what on the rim

---

[2] Unless Verne was hinting, indicating or concealing something else entirely. Michel Lamy in *Jules Verne, Initie at Initiateur* (Jules Verne, Initiate and Initiator) claims Verne's work was "entirely dedicated to the transmission of a message". Lamy claims Verne, among many other famous names, was a member of the occult 'society' known as *Le Brouillard* (mist or fog) (Godwin, 1996).

and when? And, indeed, why (see *the elder Pharos*)? The majority of Danforth and Dyer's recent shocking revelations have been conveyed to them by studying carvings of a sort (in the ancient city the history of the Earth is cut into the walls). It seems natural that any further horror should be conveyed in the same way, perhaps simply on a larger scale. Could this imply that the entire earth is simply some artificial vessel of unthinkable (perhaps lost) purpose? Did something emerge from inside the earth (see later commentary on possible inhabitants of *the black pit* and also *The Ethics of Ygor* on chthonian spaces)?

More metaphorically, Danforth's "bizarre material" often over-emphasises distance and isolation by referring to 'the rim of space' (an interesting proposition in itself, postulating that space does indeed have an end but that what comes from beyond is far worse). If the 'rim' here is contextualised with *Yog Sothoth, the colour out of space* and *the wings* then it could be possible to see the interior of the earth (or possibly, if you don't like to live so dangerously, only the pit itself of whatever size) as a vast and transgressive space. We live on a mere crust between outer space and an internal darkness beyond comprehension. Remembering that Danforth's vision may also be only a reflection *in the sky* adds resonance to this image.

The Proto-shoggoths

The shoggoths in the Dyer narrative are formless, protoplasmic slave beings called into existence in the distant past. They can be moulded (or mould themselves) into any useful living tool. The idea of a form of life on which they themselves are based seems at first glance to be somewhat redundant. They appear quite protean enough as it is. But we must remember what Danforth has been through; he has seen evidence that life on earth is an accident, some form of science experiment gone awry. His problems, from then on, are ontological and aetiological. What is this? Where has all this come from? Issues of genetic, sexual and spiritual origins are all hidden in the apparently excessive notion of proto-shoggoths, issues that obviously recur when he talks of *the primal white jelly* and, finally, *the original, the eternal, the undying.*

The Windowless Solids with five dimensions

The number five appears regularly in the Dyer narrative. It would appear to be the alien equivalent of our ten fingers at the very least, though there is some indication that their writing (mathematics?) also involves the number. As a dimension it again functions as excess – if the fourth dimension is time (debatable but taken as read here.[3]) then the fifth is even less understandable, more damaging to the limits of the mind.

A further possible connection may serve as a clue to Danforth's state of mind. As mentioned, he was a graduate student at Miskatonic University in Arkham, Mass. in the spring of 1930 before his debilitation. Two years previously another scholar, Walter Gilman, went so far as to die in unusual circumstances. He was an excellent mathematics student with great potential. His friend and

---

[3] In a sense, all previous notions of time, or at least history, have already been upset by Danforth's discoveries. Time, a previously understood and relied upon phenomenon, may be lost to them now. One is reminded of the strange nature of the ship in Poe's *MS Found in a Bottle*, with its implications of vast age and interminable journeying to the site of the Southern Pole: like the endless fall toward some earthbound event horizon of a black hole. It could also be noted that "Past, Present, Future, all are one in Yog Sothoth," according to the *Necronomicon.*

colleague, Frank Elwood, graduated from Miskatonic in June 1929. The strange circumstances surrounding Gilman's death and Elwood's short breakdown soon after have never been fully explained but both Gilman and Elwood spoke and wrote of dreams, informed by their studies of advanced dimensional mathematics, in which they saw or pictured living beings and inanimate objects as colours and prismatic shapes, all barely describable on awakening[4]. It is only this kind of concept that allows any understanding of a 'solid with five dimensions'.

'Windowless' could also imply something at least the size of a large building. Psychologically, a lack of windows betrays a fear of being inescapably caught inside, with no outside to be seen, a further dimensional excess. But again, these are solids, how would a window be even conceivable without recourse to supra-dimensional thinking, beyond simple concepts of inside and out?

All this theorising cannot fail to bring to mind the film known as *The Navidson Record*, that extraordinary documentary of the exploration of an incalculably vast space 'inside' the house on Ash Tree Lane occupied for a time by photo-journalist Will Navidson and his family: all 'windowless', all dark and apparently as changeable and unpredictable as a living thing. Although the *Record* and the Zampano narrative that accompanies it are modern documents, they do contain reference to certain earlier histories and features of the area. Lord De la Warr's personal journals and his cryptic discovery in uncharted woodland – "Ftaires! We haue found ftaires!" – in the seventeenth century are at least a matter of record although the

---

[4] It is also possible that a partial inspiration for the Old Ones was the tiny metal figure that Gilman left with the University in April 1928. It bears a significant resemblance to the creatures Danforth and Dyer saw in part and pictures only.

likelihood of Danforth having direct access to such material is small. Rumours, however, and tall tales are much harder to track. And, of course, Danforth could well have been an avid collector of such unverifiable information. Perhaps more significant is the description of the house on Ash Tree Lane given by the parapsychologist Lucinda S. Hausmaninger. She describes it as "the omphalos of all we are" (Danielewski, pg 414 - from Hausmaninger's "Oh Say Can You See" in *The Richmond Lag Zine*, v.119, April 1995, p.33).

As a psychological archetype then, the space in *The Navidson Record* may be of similar provenance to his visions but as far as Danforth's likely reading is concerned we need look no further than the manuscript discovered in 1877 by Messrs. Tonnison and Berreggnog in the ruins that lie to the south of the village of Kraighten in the West of Ireland, known as *The House on the Borderland*. Again we cannot be certain that Danforth had read this singular MS but its fame among readers of 'bizarre material' makes it highly likely that a copy may have sat on his shelves at the University.

The Borderland MS. too contains a *lacuna* like the Pym narrative but, unusually, it comes in the middle of the work. 'The Fragments', recreated from the only legible parts of the MS at this point, allude to the loss of the narrator's love/sister (this idea from Iain Sinclair's unusual reading in his 1997 introduction to the text) and his return from "that enormous darkness" which is, by implication *outside* "the known universe": two references we may have come to recognise by now.

Both the *Record* and the *House* involve 'underground' adventures that go beyond the protagonist's ability to understand or conceptualise their situation. Both force upon their hapless explorers drastic, possibly psychotic, breakdowns, calling for a personal re-evaluation of their understanding of the universe and our place in it.

Danforth and Dyer have already experienced something similar.

Danforth's reading of the Borderland MS and Gilman's papers is compelling him to attempt an understanding of the reality of what he may have seen, pushing him beyond normal thought.

The Nameless Cylinder

A ruined cylindrical building is the entrance and beginning of a descent into the first, revealed 'black pit' in the narrative (the underground sea where the shoggoths have survived). The recurrence of the description here (followed by a similar but specifically named reference, *the elder Pharos*) indicates Danforth's continuing inability to coherently describe and contain the 'objects' seen in or around *the black pit* while still retaining the inevitable notion that any genuine understanding of his visions will somehow be his downfall, laying waste to what little remains of his hold on sanity.

Poe, in *Descent into the Maelstrom*, dwells on cylinders and barrels (Dyer describes the Old Ones as barrel shaped), the two shapes that survive the whirlpool most effectively. The narrator watches them from his captured boat, studying their dynamics in the water and finally electing to cling to a barrel as the best chance of survival. Danforth's (deliberately?) disjointed recollections recall the mariner's predicament in the deep, dark whirlpool where "The rays of the moon seemed to search the very bottom of the profound gulf...". Is this also where Danforth found *the moon-ladder*? Or even the beam of *the elder Pharos*?

The Elder Pharos

The original (but younger) Pharos was the small island off the coast of the city of Alexandria on which stood a huge, for classical times, lighthouse, guiding ships into the bay. It was one of the Seven Wonders of the Ancient world and the island has become synonymous with the building. As an image of horror it is worth noting two things.

Firstly, Alexandria's more famous civic wonder was its library, a symbol now of ancient wisdom, all the more significant and enigmatic because of its destruction and the loss of its many texts. What repository of knowledge could an *elder Pharos* be directing one towards? Danforth is already overwhelmed by unwanted knowledge. Is he hinting at further steps in a dangerous direction?

Secondly, the lighthouse as a beacon for attracting, warning or directing ships. All of these options heighten the significance of *the wings,* possibly *the moon-ladder* and certainly *the colour out of space.* Modern Hollow Earth theories have not shied away from incorporating UFOs into their mythology, making free with the 'science' of polarity and magnetism, turning the Antarctic into some vast attractor, a landing area for alien craft or spiritually laden cosmic meteors[5]. Returning to the separation of the inner and outer (from *the carven rim)* some theories see craft coming from worlds inside the earth.

Yog-Sothoth

Yog Sothoth may be the key source of Danforth's terrible visions. Dyer claims to have only a little knowledge of the *Necronomicon* but is sure

---

[5] The suppressed report from the Secondary Magnetic Pole Expedition in 1938 records the discovery and destruction of just such a craft, buried in ice and the cause of magnetic disturbance for twenty million years. A possible origin for Poe's and Verne's Sphinx? (Stuart 1938)

that Danforth, on the other hand, is "among the few who have ever dared go completely through that worm-riddled copy...kept under lock and key in the college library."[6] This ancient text, as might be expected, does indeed contain important references.

Yog Sothoth is known by several descriptive names or titles, including "the key and guardian of the Gate", "the Lurker at the Threshold" and "the key to the gate, whereby the spheres meet". The 'gate' is the access point through which the Old Gods can return to earth. It may, in some sense, actually *be* Yog Sothoth as well. So although the 'gate' and its operation remain somewhat metaphysical, certain locations for it (and therefore presumably Yog Sothoth as well) are given: "Kadath in the cold waste hath known Them, and what man knows Kadath? The ice desert of the south...hold(s) stones whereon Their seal is engraven, but who hath seen the deep frozen city...?" Here there are echoes of the *carven rim* again, a 'Threshold' not to be crossed. Also "...whereby the spheres meet..." inevitably brings us back to Symmes Hollow Earth and his "number of solid concentric spheres" contained therein. A hole, the *black pit*, would be the only place where these spheres could be said to meet.

Alternatively the spheres may be other worlds – leading us back to the possible function of *the elder Pharos* and *the moon-ladder*.

---

[6] There is a substantial irony in this – "...the directors of the Library (at Miskatonic University) recognized the necessity for a secure setting for its rarities and incunabula. The Darby Room...became the Rare Book Room of the Library. A special curator, appointed on the strength of an additional endowment from the Danforth family, ensured that none of the books in the room left it and that scholars and students used them only in his presence..." (Stanley, 1993, pg 10) This occurred sometime between 1835 and 1860. Danforth may have had access to his "bizarre material" primarily because of his own family's gift in the previous century. Family is fate, as usual, *original* and *undying*.

Finally perhaps, we must simply allow that, as a potentially omnipresent god, *the original, the eternal, the undying,* Yog-Sothoth may be the source of Danforth's terrible visions.

The Primal White Jelly

No matter how much Dyer talks of shapeless shoggoths and alien flesh, it is difficult to ignore the distinct possibility that this particular charged description refers to semen. Danforth's continuing backward journey toward origins, begun in the at least partly recognisable *proto-shoggoth* phrase above, reaches its climax here. All talk of the *nameless cylinder* and an *elder Pharos* could be reassessed in a sexual light from here as well. The white against the *black pit*, combined with Poe's use of whiteness in *Pym*, reinforce a horror felt at fundamental sexuality, a horror of mindless reproduction and growth as evinced by the shoggoths. What could emerge from such *prima materia*? What could be worse than the things he has already seen? What is emerging from the pit of space?

The Color Out of Space

In June 1882 three Professors from Miskatonic University visited a farm in the hills west of Arkham. They were investigating the fall of an unusual meteorite. Their report and notes, still in the University archives, refer to a "colour out of space", a description of something from or in the meteorite that seemed unable to exist within the normal, visible spectrum of light, perhaps a prescient notion of an as yet unknown form of radiation. Danforth could easily have been aware of

126

this phrase and, if so, certainly knew of its association with bodies from space.

The Wings / The Eyes in Darkness

It seems odd that the more consideration one gives to the less specific descriptions, the less they yield possibilities for explanation and become all the more unsettling for that very reason. These last two isolated fragmentary organs betray no source but indicate movement and sentience without identification, something recognisable from the two men's earlier fear of both the Old Ones (wings) and the shoggoths (eyes).

The inhabitants of the pit in context hint at travel, of arrivals and departures – *the moon ladder, the elder Pharos, the wings* – calling to mind the scientific theories of Professor Clark Ashton Scarsdale and his researches into the ancient *Ethics of Ygor* (Copper, 1974)[7]. Scarsdale's 'Great White Space', an extra-dimensional area connecting outer space with the inside of the earth is, in appearance at least, the very opposite of Danforth's *black pit.* It is possible, however, that they could serve a similar function. In the chthonian darkness deep inside the planet, a white space is a contrasting, negative (on a human level) phenomenon. In the vast whiteness of Antarctica, *the black pit,* visually at the very least, has the same effect. Both overwhelm human thought with the incomprehensibility of space, with

---

[7] Scarsdale's work, up until this point, had a very limited audience though it is possible that Danforth would have had a particular interest precisely because of its abstruse nature. Ironically, after the disappearance of the Crosby-Patterson Antarctic expedition, also in 1930, Scarsdale himself made a short trip to the white continent in the following year to investigate certain unusual markings. At that time of course, Danforth and Dyer, aboard ship on their way home in all probability, were in no position to warn him of any dangers. Scarsdale met his own end in his own way. But one wonders if his final journey somehow began in the frozen south (Copper, 1974).

the notion that, over and above this-should-not-be, that this-should-not-be-*here*.

The Moon-ladder

As already mentioned, this odd, seemingly archaic concept could be relevant to the 'spheres' from *Yog-Sothoth* and Symmes. A specific connection to the moon opens up a whole field of references from classical Paganism to the influence of the moon on insanity. This description, unlike the previous two, is almost *too* specific to unravel in any useful way, resembling a fairytale image, undercutting the previous scientific tone - a *physical* connection to the moon? What climbs such a ladder? And in which direction?

Overall, *the color out of space, the wings, the eyes in darkness* and *the moon-ladder* create an indistinct impression of some unknown visitations, impossible to comprehend in an empirical, rational environment. This breakdown of comprehensibility reaches its peak in his last distinct utterance.

The Original, the Eternal, the Undying

Is it that by its indefiniteness it shadows forth the heartless voids and immensities of the universe, and thus stabs us from behind with the thought of annihilation, when beholding the white depths of the milky way?...is it for these reasons that there is such a dumb blankness, full of meaning, in a wide landscape of snows – a colorless, all-color of atheism from which we shrink?

Herman Melville – *Moby Dick*, 1851

In this attempt to expose the possible origins of Danforth's psychotic visions it is obvious that there is, among the several threads so far identified, an undisguised confusion between fact and fiction. Danforth defends himself against his earlier statements by claiming that what he saw was only an inaccurate reflection, further informed by his ill-advised consumption of curious texts of debatable authenticity. However, this final image – suggestive but not specific – is more indicative of his breakdown than he would care to admit. *The original, the eternal, the undying* obviously pinpoints the theme of regressive aetiology (*the proto-shoggoths, the primal white jelly*) while also highlighting the conflict (or perhaps the terrifying lack of conflict, even collusion?) between what could be called the origin of the beginning and the origin of the end. That which made us will destroy us. The source of all life is also the source of death. All without reference to any human, terrestrial concerns[8].

So, as before, Danforth has concocted his ramblings from a moment of stress, hours of unwanted revelation and a lifetime of strange reading.

Or a hole has been opened in his psyche by pressure from within (fiction, his own mind) and without (fact, the world). He has come to see both

---

[8] If Danforth had read the *Book of Eibon* (several versions of which were available in the Miskatonic University Library), especially the tale of the descent of the sorcerer Haon-Dor into the abyss called Y'qaa, then it would be simple to see how he could draw certain parallels in his desperate state. Y'qaa, a 'multidimensional' space with many entrances and exits deep in the primordial earth, much like the Great White Space and therefore *the black pit*, contains the being Ubbo-Sathla, described as "the source and the end" and is accompanied by shoggoths, providing another origin for life and hints of a related end. Is this myth the inspiration for his final vision (the most modern and complete version being Price ed. 2001)?

sides of this new pit. He cannot tell if he is looking up or down, from inside or out. His mind, just like the Earth below, constantly threatens to expose more and greater secrets at every moment.

Danforth is in fact 'stabbed from behind', as Melville puts it, by his very recourse to the apparently fictional works he has read. His 'excuse' is not good enough to let him off the hook. On some terrible level he must continue his endless round of indecision about the nature of what he may have seen.

The student's journey appears finally then as a series of stepped regressions, a return voyage (that reaches its height, ironically but necessarily, on the return to safety) towards a terrible void. The exposure of one monstrous unknown after another only serves to highlight the next horror – one set of impossible mountains, then another; one set of monsters (the Old Ones), then a worse kind (the shoggoths), then something even they can't face; one broken cylinder, then a *nameless* kind; one *pit*, then another...Until finally the regression can take no more and becomes *eternal* and *undying*, finally recognised as *the original* condition of the human mind. Even the narrative *lacunae* recur: after this examination of each of the thirteen descriptions there are still always the "other bizarre conceptions" that Dyer does not specify, leaving, as ever, another space, *pit* or hole for the imagination to fill.

There are always things that remain to be seen.

Danforth is awake when Dyer comes to visit him for the fifth time. The boy looks haggard. He has lost weight and his pupils are like pinpricks, anti-stars in the blue sky of his eyes. But he smiles when the Professor appears. The shutters on the window are open. Daylight, hot and sane, illuminates the ward.

130

"Hello Sir, thank you for coming again. I apologise for the burden I must have been to you for the last few months".

Dyer pauses. Being addressed like that, as of old, being apologised to in such a formal and, it must be said, obviously rehearsed manner, is not the reception to which he has become accustomed. He sits, nodding, and accepts the tea proffered by a silent and obliging nurse. He has been informed by the Doctors involved that Danforth is 'as well as we can hope' and that he has requested to be sent home to his family rather than continue his studies at Miskatonic. He will need constant supervision and a regulated drug intake to remain calm. He is, they are sorry to say, an addict by now but this, they add, may be for the best. Danforth, still smiling, continues.

"I hope I have not alarmed you in any way. I understand that I have not been well. I realise that I may have communicated things to you that were not... true. When I was sick. Everything I said, it was all... I mean, it is all... Sir, I read it. It was in books, horrible books, books that make no sense, what's the word?" Danforth's eyes close for a second. Dyer looks around nervously for the nurse. Then they open again. Still the same darkness at the centre but small, overwhelmed. "Hallucinations. Fictions. All a lot of fiction. I don't know why I got so overwrought. I assure you, I will not be reading for a long while. Certainly not the kind of material...available at the University. I shall rest. Rest and put it all behind me. Thank you for your support while I've been in here. I'm glad you came

131

when... when you did. Things to get off my chest. Clear it up. Cleared up. All gone now. But enough of me, I'm being so rude. How have you been?"

For a moment Dyer feels only the loss of a fine student. Then he looks down into his cup. The white rim, the darkness inside, movement beneath, the dregs, the end, the pit.

Outside, the sun dims.

Bibliography

Blavatsky, Helena Petrovna – ***The Origin of Evil*** – Theosophical Publishing House, Adyar, 1917 – ***The Secret Doctrine*** – 2 vols, Theosophical Publishing House, 1888.

Cannon, Peter – ***The Chronology Out of Time: Dates in the Fiction of H.P.Lovecraft*** – Necronomicon Press, 1986.

Carter, Angela – ***Lovecraft and Landscape*** – in ***The Necronomicon***, Neville Spearman, 1978, ed. George Hay

Collins, Paul – ***Banvard's Folly*** – Picador, 2001 – the chapter on Symmes is also reprinted in ***Fortean Times 153***, December 2001 and ***McSweeney's***, Vol. 12.

Copper, Basil – ***The Great White Space*** – Robert Hale, 1974.

Danielewski, Mark Z. – ***House of Leaves*** – Pantheon, 2000.

Godwin, Joscelyn – ***Arktos: the Polar Myth in Science, Symbolism and Nazi Survival*** – Adventures Unlimited Press, 1996.

Hodgson, William Hope – ***The House on the Borderland***, 1908.

Lovecraft, Howard Phillips – ***At The Mountains of Madness***, 1936, ***Dreams in the Witch House,*** 1933, ***The Dunwich Horror***, 1929, ***The Colour Out of Space***, 1927– in Arkham House collection ***The Outsider and Others,*** 1939.

Maroney, Tim – **The Book of Dzyan**, Chaosium, 2000.

Melville, Herman – **Moby Dick, or The Whale**, 1851.

Poe, Edgar Allan – **The Narrative of Arthur Gordon Pym of Nantucket**, 1838 – Penguin 1975 (this edition also contains extracts from Jules Verne's **Le Sphinx de Glaces**, 1897) – also **MS Found in a Bottle** and **Descent into the Maelstrom.**

Price, Robert M. (selected and introduced by) – **The Book of Eibon**, Chaosium 2001.

Stanley, Joan C. – **Ex Libris Miskatonici – A Catalogue of Selected Items from the Special Collections in the Miskatonic University Library** – Necronomicon Press, 1993.

Stuart, Don A. (John W. Campbell Jnr) – **Who Goes There?** – 1938, in **SF Hall of Fame – The Novellas**, ed. Ben Bova, Gollancz 1973.

Washington, Peter – **Madame Blavatsky's Baboon**, Secker & Warburg, 1993.

LOVECRAFT, LACAN AND THE LURKING FEAR

The world changed fast. Johnny ignored school for bikes, booze, birds, pills, and smoke, in that order. And he read a lot. He lifted books by Lovecraft from local racks.

Alex R. Stuart
The Devil's Rider.

In the beginning was *The Outsider*. And it was without form. The story tells of a being with no sense of its own origins or nature, living in perpetual twilight in a gloomy castle surrounded by forbidding trees. No light, stars, moon or sun are ever seen, nor has the creature anything but vague intimations of its own self – as there are no 'others'.

> *Such a lot the Gods gave to me – to me, the dazed, the disappointed, the barren, the broken. And yet I am strangely content and cling desperately to these sere memories when my mind momentarily threatens to reach beyond to the other.*

Finally driven to suicide (by what? Traditional Romantic notions I'd wager. But I digress), it finds itself in a new place, unnerved and lost. In the company of others it finds itself in the reflection of a mirror. The action releases knowledge of self.

The Outsider resembles the Kleinian child, which the archetypal French psychoanalyst, Jacques Lacan, describes as a "fragmented body"[1] and which appears in dreams and analysis as "an aggressive disintegration of the individual"[2]. The mirror gives limits, form and recognition. In Lovecraft this process subjects the creature to a release of memory during which it (in this pre-gendered, pre-Oedipal state the child/monster has no sexual identity in theory or story) accepts itself for what it is seen to be and, in doing so, loses any fear.

> *In the supreme horror of that second I forgot what had horrified me, and in the*

burst of black memory vanished in a
chaos of echoing images.

Finally it flees "in a dream".

On closer inspection, *The Outsider* exhibits
further parallels as a metaphor for the initial stages
of child development. It speaks of youth and a lack
of speech. If speech came (which, apart from one
'ghastly ululation', it never does), in Lacanian terms
it would signify an entrance into the Symbolic Order
and the beginnings of the formulation of the classic
Oedipal triangle. In the story this is not to be; the
subject/child/monster remains in the Imaginary
which, "is equivalent to becoming psychotic and
incapable of living in human society"[3]. So the
Outsider's appearance brings, in 'human society', "a
sudden and unheralded fear of hideous intensity"
leaving it free to "play by day amongst the
catacombs of Nephren-Ka..." In the following
description of a new life, echoes can also be heard of
Lacan's suggested dream symbolization of the
formation of subject's 'I'(dentity);

> *I know that light is not for me, save that*
> *of the moon over the rocky tombs of Neb,*
> *nor any gaiety save the unnamed feasts*
> *of Nitokris beneath the Great Pyramid.*
>
> -Lovecraft

> *...a fortress, or a stadium – its inner area*
> *and closure surrounded by marshes and*
> *rubbish tips, dividing it into two opposed*
> *fields of conquest where the subject*
> *flounders in quest of the lofty, remote*
> *inner castle...*
>
> -Lacan[4]

The motivating emotions mentioned in the
two passages provoke an even more curious
parallel: in Lacan's scenario, which is presumably
symptomatic of a problematized situation, the

subject 'flounders in quest', whereas the Outsider appears to accept his 'remote inner castle' as an entirely appropriate home and indeed exhibits a bitter acceptance of his dark nature, seeing 'gaiety' in unnamed feasts.

Lastly, the narrative structure itself is not enclosed in a construct that explains its own existence. It does not purport to be a diary or a warning or even a manuscript. It could not be, because it is the work of a monster, an outsider, a psychotic who has not yet gained proper access to language, telling a story which pre-"dates...the deflection of the specular 'I' in to the social 'I'".[5]

> It resurfaces, it troubles, it turns the presents feeling of being "at home" into an illusion, it lurks – this "wild", the "ob-scene", this "filth", this "resistance" of "superstition" – within the walls of residence, and, behind the back of the owner (the ego), or over its objections, it inscribes there the law of the other.

-Michel de Certeau

Could you get more specific about the type of horror Lovecraft evokes?

The next stage of development is the entry of the child into the Symbolic Order. This involves the intrusion of the Father into the mother/child dyad and the initiation of the child into language. It is this process which occasions the production of the unconscious while also explaining its structure (as "reflecting" language). The Symbolic Order is the patriarchal construct which separates, in its societally marked definitions, the "child" from the "mother", which orders that "desire must wait, that it must formulate in the constricting word whatever demand it may speak"[6.] This destroys the illusory completeness of the child's imaginary ego. There is no longer the illusion that all desires can be satisfied and instead they become helplessly structured by external relations and are therefore, inherently, unfulfilled. It is this awful gap, the gap between the demand for the "perfection" of fulfilled desire and the restricting structures of language that force an unconscious into existence.

But the speech of the subject, his definition as being, is dependent on and continually invaded by traces of that imaginary, the discourse of the Other; "...its frenzy mocking the abyss of the infinite..."[7]. That was Lacan by the way, not Lovecraft. It is part of Lacan's description of the nature of desire in the language-ridden subject, when, with "elusive ambiguity the ring of meaning flees from our grasp along the verbal thread."[8]

> *There is nothing in the unconscious which accords with the body. The unconscious is discordant. The unconscious is that which, by speaking, determines the subject as being, but as being to be crossed through with that metonymy by which I support desire, in so far as it is endlessly impossible to speak as such.*

-Lacan[9]

So that, it seems, is the paradox of speaking. It is the only way left for the unconscious to communicate and yet in doing so, by the very use of language itself, it cannot achieve its desired aim. This also provides some insight into why the unconscious is sometimes seen as primal, old, basic and dark, something almost left behind (although Lacan does resist this view; he does not see the unconscious as the seat of human drives). The subject will be accepted in society through language, on condition that desires are perpetually curbed by language at the same time.

Lacan also says "the truth is always disturbing. We cannot even manage to get used to it. We are used to the real. The truth we repress"[10]. Which seems, uncharacteristically and somewhat unnervingly, quite clear for a change.

In Lovecraft, the actions of his subjects/protagonists, initially well within the Symbolic order of normal, scientific, historical discourses, bring them inevitably closer to the "truth". The explorers in the Antarctic, the projects of the various scientists, the genealogical quests of young men, all lead them ever forward – to the past. In the city of the Old Ones a scientific origin is hinted at. In Lacan "...the slightest alteration in the relation between man and signifier, in this case the procedures of exegesis, changes the whole course of history by modifying the moorings which anchor his being".[11]

It is these "procedures of exegesis" (which, once written, tend to be fatal to sanity, then life) that Lovecraft's protagonists inevitably execute and undergo at the same time. On contact with the "true" nature of things, they die, go mad or retire from life[12]. The cosmic horror so appreciated by Lovecraft is at the very nature of the universe in actuality. The (arguably) ultimate God of the Mythos, Azathoth – a psychoanalytic nightmare if ever there was one – consists of several disparate and almost arbitrary descriptions: scientific ("monstrous nuclear chaos beyond angled space"), poetic ("mindless Daemon-sultan") and downright insulting ("blind idiot god" – although that has made for a fine band name). So the "arcana of basic entity" is being brought very close to the surface of consciousness (and to the page) by these men and their strange desires. Even the *Necronomicon* is reliably clear on just how unavoidably and definitively close disruption by unconscious forces can be. In fact it is quite specific about the two sites at which you can count on being troubled: where language is created and in the home. Remember: "Their hand is at your throats yet ye see them not; and Their habitation is even one with your guarded threshold".

So these monstrosities are forever close, primal and defining, always ready to disrupt the social discourse of the protagonist in much the same way as the unconscious can be seen to disrupt and inhabit the psyche of the subject.

The fear of knowledge, of facing the repressed of both private mind and public body, the final confrontation, is articulated as the crisis point in in the protagonists own narration.

So what am I saying?

What happens when you come right up against your "guarded threshold" and take it right to where "they" live?

> *If I have said that the unconscious is the discourse of the other... it is in order to indicate the beyond in which the recognition of desire for recognition... In other words the other is the Other that even my lie invokes as a guarantor of the truth in which it subsists... By which we can also see it is with the appearance of language the dimension of truth emerges.*
>
> -Lacan[13]

> *The words reaching the reader can never even suggest the awfulness of the sight itself.*
>
> -Lovecraft

The majority of the stories are narrated in the first person and are usually given some fictional framework to explain their existence – a warning, a statement, a "test of my own sanity" and so on. If any useful parallel with Lacanian psychoanalysis is relevant then at the critical encounters with Mythos creatures there should necessarily be some equally critical disruption in language as the "subject" comes face to 'face' with the return of the unthinkable. And, indeed, "Poor Johansen's handwriting almost gave out when he wrote of this."

At almost every climactic moment language is not up to the strain. Robert Blake's diary descends into disjointed poetics at the point of identification. The alien nature of the Mythos names takes them outside normal human speech and pronunciation. In both *At the Mountains of Madness* and *The Case of Charles Dexter Ward*, protagonists slip into mad litany combined with a psychotic inability to focus on the object in question, one reciting underground stations and the other revealing Lovecraft's opinion of Modernist poetry.

Ironically, but perhaps necessarily from a psychoanalytic point of view, it is language and the Symbolic Order which seduce Lovecraft's protagonists to begin their disastrous quests. They encounter the first threads of the Other in language: through the huge library of real and unreal books or the archaic archives of their forerunners. Following the paper trails left by ancestors and authors of forbidden books, the investigator is finally driven to confront what the trial (oops, sorry, trail) of language has continually hinted at, only to find that it is beyond language, the discourse of the Other made evident. At which point, as Angela Carter puts it, dementia ensues or, faced with unacceptable truth, suicide is chosen[12]. Once the quest has begun, its end is inevitable. When you start to write, you have already lost.

The truth of writing, the truth behind the hints in the books, the truth of the confessions and the warnings is that the truth cannot be expressed in writing, by language. It cannot be owned, contained, expressed or even adequately

142

communicated. If you get too close, it will exile you from sane and proper communication forever. You will feel their hand at your throat.

But even here the surviving narrators draw back. Or, at least, their language does. In all the stories that do not result in sudden death, the truth is still never directly stated. Albert Wilmarth runs in terror from the "face and hands of Henry Wentworth Akeley" whose position, *sans* body, on a chair, proves that he has spent all night talking to a disguised alien whose existence, now undeniably proven, he never admits to in plain words.[14] The narrator of *Mountains of Madness* continually wishes only to hint at certain inevitable conclusions that must be reached by the reader and not laid down in words. The patently obvious has never been so devious.

On a few occasions even those alien races which afford the initial horror are allowed to become recognizable as sane and sentient only when they become victims of another fear which cannot be faced. The Old Ones face the degenerate shoggoths in *Mountains* (there are even secondary summits hinted at in the end) and the Great Race face the Flying Polyps in *Shadow Out of Time*.

In every story there is a limit that cannot be crossed, a barrier that cannot and should not be breached – but its very existence defines the crisis of language and sanity in which the narrators find themselves: "I am forced into speech..."

There is a further paper trial to follow, to lead us again simultaneously toward and away from whatever fearful truth may be out there. American Surrealists wrote on Lovecraft as early as 1943. Lacan read and contributed to French surrealist magazines and journals in the forties.[15] Did he encounter traces of Lovecraft? Did he read Levy's biography in 1969? Is that another story?

Dare I continue?

Notes and Bibliography

1. From analyst Melanie Klein: Lacan's description from 'The Mirror Stage' in *Ecrits: A Selection* (Tavistock 1977).
2. Ibid, pg 4.
3. Toril Moi, *Sexual/Textual Politics* (Methuen 1985), pg 100.
4. 'The Mirror Stage', pg 5.
5. Michel de Certeau, *Heterologies: Discourse on the Other* (Manchester University Press, 1986), pg 4.
6. Elizabeth Wright, *Psychoanalytic Criticism: Theory in Practice* (Methuen 1984), pg 109.
7. From 'The Agency of the Letter in the Unconscious', *Ecrits*, pg 166.
8. Ibid.
9. Lacan, 'Seminar of 21st January 1975' in *Feminine Sexuality*, eds. Juliet Mitchell and Jacqueline Rose (Macmillan 1983), pg 165.
10. 'Agency of the Letter...' pg 169.
11. Ibid, pg 174.
12. Except, of course, in *Shadow Over Innsmouth*, the magnificent tale which largely undermines my entire thesis.
13. 'Agency of the Letter...' pg 172.
14. This is, as has been pointed out to me, extremely debatable. Whose fantasy of 'plain words' could be appealed to here? Language is seducing someone: me, Lovecraft, the narrator? I can't decide.
15. David Macey, *Lacan in Contexts* (Verso 1988).

*

This essay would have been impossible without the able assistance of Dr. Vicky Lebeau who told me to

144

drop all the stuff about Freud. Which I did. The sections where I might give the impression of understanding Jacques Lacan are down to her and the sections where I talk rubbish are all my own work. Thanks are also due to Robert Price for being interested.

1987/1997/2013

I wrote this a long time ago. Putting aside a sincere and heartfelt lack of academic credibility on my part, I still enjoy the bits where Lacan sounds as barmy as Howard. Perhaps that was the only point I was making.

SIGNS & SIGNALS

I got a paper cut when I opened Sean's letter, another thing that hurts more than you would expect. Sucking my own blood, I shook off his dangerous envelope and flapped the single sheet open. Sean had not forgotten me for some reason, even though I hadn't thought of him in five years. His letter, in among the nonsense, contained an invitation to stay at a house he owned on the coast of north Cornwall, a place called Trefoil. He took up were we had left off, as if nothing had happened in the time since we had left London. I was pleased.

Sean Crane never finished his degree. I imagine he didn't care much, then or now. He left abruptly in his third year, causing only slight concern among his few friends. I happened to know that he had been having some kind of family trouble for some time before his unexpected departure but he never gave any warning, even to me. He had not been specific about his home life at all; but I only realised this after he had gone.

Fascinating as he was to me, most people shied away, made timid by his abrasive personality and nervous of his interests. Ostensibly an artist, he produced massive and highly successful works that were deliberately dangerous. His favourite were the billboards installed on roadsides that were simply huge photographs of harmless turnings, put there in the hope that one day someone would drive into one by mistake. Some rich members of the art community loved pampering this nonsense, others, including most of his tutors, found it annoying. At least that's what they claimed. Naturally his sales and success had no part in their enmity. Besides, he did not care about that. He didn't care about his art very much at all.

The pebbles under here, in the shade of the upturned boat, look new. Some have been smashed apart revealing jagged sharp lines. Others appear melted together by intense heat, meaningless lumps shot through with carbonised seaweed. I found one

148

with a fish emerging from it. It appeared to have been swimming through rock quite successfully for a while before it was thrown up on this novel stretch of seabed. Rock like liquid, still capable of supporting a kind of life. I am hiding under here, hiding from it all. They cannot see me.

No, Sean did not care about art, he was more interested in the occult, first alchemy then what he called 'hidden designs'. His art actually made a kind of sense once you knew this about him but people rarely got that far. One night, when we were drunk, he told me that his father claimed to have met Fulcanelli.

"Who?"

"A modern day version of St Germain," he said, swinging his empty pint glass between two fingers.

"Oh," I replied. "Actually, no," I continued when I had fetched fresh beer, "I give in. Who the hell are you talking about?"

"The Comte de St Germain was first sighted..."

"No, no, I know about him, ageless, keeps popping up in the seventeenth and eighteenth centuries, claims all sorts of infernal knowledge, probably became a good alias for all those dodgy jokers who wanted to impress women at Royal Courts in Europe. No, Fulcanelli."

"Don't confuse me. If you're not sober enough to continue a conversation, then piss off. Anyway, they are similar in some ways. Fulcanelli may have written two books on the occult secrets of Cathedrals: he was very taken with the magic of architecture. He may also have been a group of Parisian occultists writing under an assumed name. Or one of them. Whatever. He may still be living in Florence to this day. None of that matters. He claimed that the secrets of alchemy were hidden in the designs of cathedrals. At least, that's what he wrote in the two books that were published. There was a third. It may be that even all that work, the first two books, was just a front, covering more secrets. That was how my father thought; the secret significance of obvious structures absorbed both of us in the end. I think that was why he talked to my Dad actually, he just saw through all the deception. It didn't matter if this freak really was old man Fulcanelli or not, what mattered was the work."

"How'd you get into it then?"

"Well, it was what I wasn't supposed to know about, of course. He hid it from me, like Christmas presents. Except Christmas never came until I forced it."

Deception. Legend placed Lyonnesse, the secret land, out under the sea, hidden. Do you see? Legend hid it in the sea. That's not where it really is. Sean always forced things, pushed things too far.

I liked him. I had some interest in the occult myself. We fought over books in the library that no one else had touched for years. We argued, quite soberly, about the misrepresentation of occult science in the academic communities of the seventeenth century. Even when we were out, we only talked about this kind of thing: shouting about Hermes Trismegistus and Aristotle in a bar is not liable to make you many friends. So I saw other people without Sean around. I don't think he saw anyone; he would just make the odd trip down to the West Country to stay at his parents place. He never came back from these visits refreshed or happy. In fact, he was normally more edgy and sensitive afterwards. I wondered why he bothered.

Then, one day, he didn't come back.

I was concerned but not enough to take official enquiries any further. The University simply said he had dropped out and wouldn't be finishing any courses for the final year. Personally I was more intrigued than offended but exams loomed and not having an awkward friend like Sean around was, in the end, an advantage. Life went on.

Life still does for the moment. But what goes on behind it? What if the warships massing off the coast begin a surely ineffectual bombardment of... this place? They too are hidden behind the white horizon. Can the cliffs see that far? Can they see me, this close?

I drove down at the earliest opportunity suggested. I had the time and I was bored. Sean's letter reminded me of exciting times, interesting thoughts, back before the age of dull jobs. He had, with that awkwardness I well remembered, failed to enclose a phone number of any sort. But that didn't matter. Truth is I wanted to see Sean again. It all came back to me after the paper cut; the excitement, the weird talks, the books, all that nonsense that seemed so important then. Nowadays I may have known that what was lost was unimportant, but it was still, with hindsight, far more fun.

Dartmoor, green grass and smooth grey rock, passed. Cornish houses are black, ugly things that shine in the rain or are painted white in a kind of desperation. I try not to think about the scenery. I don't want to imagine what has become of it. All the roads looked the same near the coast. Outside Trefoil, a tiny village of five houses, shop and pub, Sean's house was up on the cliffs. There were none of the torturous winding ways down to the old fishing villages to negotiate. Two lefts and a right, then a wide drive and, beneath the blue sky, a house like all the others. The only house with a police car outside it. Oh Sean. I pulled up, got out of the car. The blue sky had been hiding a cold wind all the while. I did my coat up automatically and chose between knocking on the door of the house or the police car.

The young officer jerked awake, spilling coffee over his uniform.

"Jesus... Oh look at that, shit... Yes, can I help you sir?" At least that's what I imagine he said.

151

He repeated the last of it when he thought to wind down the window. I asked him if Sean Crane was at home and why he was there. With nothing more than a puzzled look he took me into the house. The door was open. Another man came downstairs -not Sean, of course- looked quizzically at the damp officer who stammered some excuse, then motioned me to sit down. A man of few words I gathered.

Sean's parlour reminded me of caravans from the seventies, all Formica tops and mismatched crockery. I found it comforting but perhaps everyone of a certain age does. It did not look like it had seen any use for some time. Only the kettle could be considered new. Coffee, I remembered, was one of Sean's main addictions. The man from upstairs indicated a chair as the younger officer, shamefaced, returned to his car.

"Can I ask what you are doing here, Sir?" he said, placing both palms flat on the table and managing to sound irritated at my unexpected arrival. He acted like I had interrupted something. I told him my name and fumbled for Sean's letter, needing legitimacy in the face of authority. He managed to read it without betraying anything at all.

"I see. Did you speak to Mr Crane recently?"

"No. In fact, I haven't spoken to him for quite a few years and, as you can see, there's no phone number. Is there a phone here?"

"No. Mr Crane is not here."

"Uh, yes, alright. What do you mean exactly? Where has he gone?"

"We don't know. He has disappeared."

I took the letter back, noticing the dark stain in the corner. The policeman said nothing further. Like getting blood from a stone. Blood on paper. The water in the sea begins to thicken, glowing white, a beacon. Don't think about that.

He sighed, lifting his hands, finally deciding to tell me more. Sean had been living down here for over a year; kept, as they say, himself to himself but was not averse to a drink with the locals on occasion. Said he was doing a great deal of research. People round here knew his family quite well. Three days ago he failed to pick up his weekly groceries. When the police arrived this morning, the front door was unlocked. Nothing of value was taken, there were no signs of a break in but the study where he must have worked was a mess. The inspector added that he could not tell if this last point was evidence of anything other than an untidy mind.

The strangest thing was that I felt little surprise at any of this. It just seemed to fit in with Sean so well. The awkwardness of my position, the slight frisson of danger, the fact that none of it made much sense: this was how Sean could make people feel, how he liked them to feel. This trick could be being played on me.

The Inspector smiled.

"Will you be staying here?"

"I suppose so. I mean, is there any reason I shouldn't? Do you expect him to turn up?"

"I have no idea. What do you think?"

"Might he have gone to see his parents? They live round here, you said they were..."

"They own a lot of land. We couldn't trace Mr. Crane senior from one day to the next I'm afraid. He may even be abroad."

"Oh. Do they own this house?"

"Certainly."

"I was under the impression Sean owned it."

"He gave you the wrong impression then, I'm afraid."

The Inspector left me to my own thoughts after that. As he and his deputy drove away, I looked out over the landscape. It stopped abruptly about two hundred yards behind the house, plummeting down to the rocks and the sea. The wind farm dominated the headland to the north.

White blades turned slowly, slower than you might expect, heads shifting to catch the air flow, twisting down the shafts to turbines embedded in the land, in the flesh. No. Watching. Hypnotic. Watched. Can't see them anymore.

I turned away. Perhaps it was time to brave Sean's study, look for clues. Find out secrets.

There may have been no sign of a struggle as far as the police were concerned but untidy did not cover it. Books in piles on the floor, files open, half empty, papers strewn on the desk, over the keyboard of an ageing computer. I pushed these aside and turned it on.

"...geological report from 1935 states nothing of any... indications of further developments after, more than binding the wind-walker... my own attempts should be enough but... F thinks he actually is Fulcanelli..."

The documents file contained only a series of notes on disparate subjects: North American legends of the Wendigo, a demon of the winter winds and histories of Cornwall concerning the lost land of Lyonesse, supposedly somewhere off the Cornish coast or down by the Isles of Scilly to the south. And a file with my name on it.

I expected it to be empty, part of Sean's continuing joke, but it wasn't. I had never seen such a detailed family history; annotated with references to further books that I knew were not about genealogy. Sean had been trying to trace something in my bloodline. Something to do with magic. The file gave no indication that he had found anything – of course he hadn't, I am not special, surely?- but the books mentioned were way out of my league. How long had he been at this? The file only began seven months ago. Why me?

I picked up a piece of paper at random, just to avoid looking at my name on the screen. It was part of a downloaded technical guide to the wind farm up the road. Output figures, tolerances and stress experiments. The copyright contained the name Crane. I closed my surprise file, toyed with deleting it, but moved onto the net. It didn't take long.

The Crane family owned the wind farm. Built in the late seventies, it was a small but well placed and efficient example of early green technology. It had been held up as an example of the future but it was getting old now. Sean's father, apparently, was considering closing it down or selling it. I turned the computer off. Looking over the screen, the window showed half sky, half drying green grass. A brown track led over the edge of the cliff, a way down to the sea perhaps. No turning back.

Obviously the police would have looked there. And there was no indication that Sean was suicidal. Crazy perhaps, obsessed, difficult; all these things I knew. It occurred to me that Sean had never had a normal life; he had never had those last five years of boredom that made me so excited to hear from him again. He had been busy all that time. Busy with all this.

"...latitude and time, F has already solved that years ago but the nature of the sacrifice... resonance within granite cores (reported as approaching footsteps?)... no indications for several hundred years, the Akashic Records are the only memory left... one of the few locations open to influence after the purge..."

I felt compelled to visit the wind farm. The only other thing was to look over the edge of the cliff and I couldn't face that. I was taking the easy option. Sean, if this was all deliberate, had succeeded in unnerving me to such a degree that I couldn't sit still. There were too many pieces of this puzzle already. I would keep gathering them up into a vast unmanageable mess, just like Sean's room. No time to stop and think.

In the car, looking through the windshield at the white propellers, I imagined an explanation that

155

made me laugh. Was this a piece of art? Some drama, a happening, happening to me? Secret cameras in the house? At the farm? Actors for policemen? Edited together to form a stumbling collage of my confusion? All that occult nonsense, the disappearance, the letter out of the blue; all that with me as the centrepiece?

No.

Well, not quite.

Up close, the machines are even more impressive. They appear slower. It begins to seem more likely that they create the wind themselves. I stared up at them. Pylons of artificial grace. Waiting.

There was a non-descript concrete building at the entrance to the farm. It had an incongruous sign outside. Coloured in by some small child, a twisted arrow pointed to the Wind Farm Activity Centre, to where gaymes and activitees could be had. I suppose it was someone's idea of fun. At the desk, covered with postcards, plastic toys, pencils and erasers, a middle-aged woman was talking to thin air. She smiled when she saw me and raised a finger, indicating that I should wait

"Hello, what can I do for you?" she finally said, in an accent clearly not from the West Country.

"Finished your call?" I tapped my ear. I can't stand mobile phones. Like everyone has so much more to say these days. She took no notice of the minor sarcasm. I asked if she had seen Mr Crane recently.

"Which one?"

"Either."

"Well, Mr Crane is not an easy man to pin down and I've been told that little Sean is missing. Would you like a tour of the Farm, there's one due to start in ten minutes. Mind you, you are the only one here at the moment. They're expecting a storm later tonight apparently. Best stay indoors." I had

156

no intention of staying long. If she couldn't help me, I would go into the village.

Just then a car pulled up alongside mine. A big man got out. He was big in every way, tall, bulky and with a shocking amount of hair for someone in their fifties at least. I thought he was going to have to duck when he came through the door. He said hello to June, who gave him the same smile she had given me, not friendly, just automatic. I should have known. I should have guessed then. So much. So much I didn't want to know. He looked from June to me and back again. June nodded. He smiled. This too was big, splitting his face like ripe fruit.

"Frank Littlesmith." He said, extending a bear's paw, "I'm the engineer round here. Like the tour?" I said I wasn't interested; I'd come here looking for someone.

"Of course. Sean Crane no doubt. Do you know what? I don't think you're going to see him yet."

"What do you mean?"

"He's not ready."

"I'm sorry but what does that mean? What do you know about it? Have you spoken to his father?"

Littlesmith laughed. I felt the need to cover my ears.

"Oh yes, we talk, now and again. See you later." With that he disappeared behind the desk into a back room before I could formulate a sensible question. June smiled again but this time I felt she was laughing at me.

"Don't mind him. He's like that all the time. You'll get used to it."

"Thanks but I don't think I want to. You have no idea how I could contact Sean's father?"

"Oh, he'll be around, don't you worry."

I left. I would have slammed the door but instead it resisted and swung shut with more poise than I managed. I wasn't about to go to the village now, not if this was an example of what the locals were like. I had had enough of these gaymes. On the drive back I realised that Littlesmith had not asked my name. It didn't seem to matter. My presence now was merely amusing.

Back at the house I took a last look at some of Sean's papers. There was a pile of notes in someone else's handwriting. Sean had scrawled 'F' at the top. They seemed more historical than the other material, being concerned with something called "the elder Pharos". The location of this fabled monument had been deliberately falsified in some accounts, the notes claimed. Sean realised that 'F' had found it somewhere around here or as the document put it, "divined the presence".

The sea glows. I do not want to watch or remember.

I fell asleep. F laughs at me. He makes the ground tremble. The wind is fierce; the land is fallen away. Something terrible is caged but worse is coming. The whiteness begins. Sean is dead now. I am alone down here, cowering. I have been forced over the edge.

When I woke up it was dark. The wind was strong. Low in the sky, black clouds raced along the sea, driven by the unceasing wind. I looked round, into corners, expecting to see hidden cameras, as if that would make sense. I was hungry. The comforting kitchen had everything. An old bread knife next to a wooden board that had seen too many meals, a fridge with cheese and ham, half a loaf of sliced bread, butter, even some salad leaves but I couldn't be bothered with them. I had almost taken a bite of the sandwich before I remembered what the policeman had said about Sean's groceries. Three days? This food was not three days old. The bread would surely be stale by now. I bit down. Unfortunately, the sandwich was fine.

I had had enough. I wasn't going to go to the police round here. I could drive into Camborne or

Redruth soon enough, even if it was late. What the hell was that Inspector's name? Had he even told me?

The wind outside was constant and carried broken noise with it, out to sea. It blew from the north. I was worried in case trees should be blown down. Only trees. That was all I was worried about.

Over the fields, the white metal windmills turned, keeping up with the gale. I stopped the car at the turn off to the wind farm. The nine long bones had been thrown; their heads faced different directions, inwards, focused on something. The wind threw snatches of human voices at me. I regret no particular decision. None made any difference. Impossible to go back. What is behind leads you on. I drove through the wind toward the light.

A single spotlight shone across the ground. Between the pylons thirty, a hundred, people stood around a metal scaffold, twenty feet high. A single pole rose from its centre, up into the night sky, disappearing out of the light's range. The construction seemed pathetic surrounded by the vast wind towers. I got out of the car and was flung against the hood by the force of the gale. Shielding my watering eyes I tried hard to identify anyone. The sharp black shadows of four pylons swept off across the fields, to become lost in the bright green night. There was something unreal about the people; they moved but seemed relaxed, unconcerned by the violent storm. I stepped between the two nearest pylons. The terrible wind shut off instantly. Inside was calm and still. Initially, the only sound was the regular throbbing of the blades turning above, all impossibly in phase. Then I made out the murmur of voices, like an auditorium waiting for the lights to go down. I was only ten feet from the back row of people. One man looked over his shoulder at me and smiled. It was the policeman who had spilt coffee. He began to move forward through the crowd.

I looked back at my car. In the dimness I began to imagine the wind was making it rock. Soon it might be caught up in some incredible tornado. I wondered how the sea looked below the cliffs. Thrashing, enraged. I stayed inside.

Frank Littlesmith approached me from the crowd.

"I told you we'd see you soon. Just couldn't resist. He was right about you I suppose."

"What is going on?"

He drew a breath, smiling, pleased with himself.

"A great deal. A very great deal. More, in point of fact, than a lot of these people here realise. But I think, with a little prompting, you'll pick it up for yourself." He raised an arm, waving toward the spotlight, pointing upwards.

The light left the people on the ground, moved up the central pole on the scaffold. Eventually, thirty feet further up, against a background of turning blades, the crucified figure of a man.

I asked a very stupid question. But I had been being slow all day I soon realised.

"It's my son," said the man beside me. F for Father, the liar, the madman. Crane, Fulcanelli, Littlesmith.

Sean, up in the sky.

"It took years to get this far. An enormous amount of forward planning. Just for this night, in this particular place. All to bind the wind for a moment. For a purpose. You see? And still," he looked at me, "still certain secrets. Sean realised his central role a few years back. Do you know what he did about it? Can you guess?"

The blades were moving quicker. A dozen of the locals surrounded the scaffold, chanting. One of them was the Inspector, another, the woman June. I couldn't help thinking that English people don't chant; they don't believe in anything that much. It sounded ridiculous. I looked away, outside the light, into the storm. An uprooted tree passed by, for all the world like tumbleweed in a desert and as slow. My car had gone. All this delighted the man beside me. He spoke of how the wind-walker would be drawn here, to this placid island, and bound for a time, just long enough to do the work required, to set up the vibrations in the earth, then tear away the surfaces, exposing the hidden reality.

"But this is all too theoretical, too abstract for the time being, I would imagine. Let me tell you something you can understand instead. When Sean realised his life was meant for this moment, he tried to find an alternative, a replacement. He thought of you. I allowed him to think you were an acceptable substitute; it kept him close. It's good to be remembered, isn't it?"

Suddenly the storm was in there with us. The pole rocked back and forth. The blades sliced a pale mist, which finally reformed around Sean, thickening until he was invisible. The noise of the unnatural gale meant we could hear neither chanting nor screaming. The ground began to shake. Some of the people were shocked. Frightened, they ran toward the concrete Activity Centre. Cracks appeared in the walls before any reached it. Many were thrown to the ground by the movement of the earth; others were blown down. Inevitably, a piercing metallic scream stood out in the confusion. One of the pylons began to shear at its base. The collapse crushed the spotlight. The last thing I noticed was the top of the scaffold pole before it fell. The mist had dissipated. The body had gone.

Sean's father, hair covering his face, braced against the wind, screamed in my ear, "Congratulate me, congratulate me."

So here I am, on the new beach. Hiding from the gaze of things newly exposed. I ran, like all the others. Out into the night, trying to avoid the fissures opening up in the landscape, trying not to think about the light and the noises coming from some of them. I found myself almost back at the house. I would like to say the storm and the earthquake drove me over the cliff edge, onto the tiny path down to the beach but I don't truly remember. Perhaps there is something about me, something only Sean knew. Why climb down a cliff when they are falling down around you? But I was, as a result, afforded a fine view of the family's success.

Halfway down the cliff face, I looked out to sea. Dawn was coming. The sea had moved away from the shore, much further than the lowest tide and in only the time it took me to climb down this far. Black seaweed crisped from some internal heat. Steam rose from the exposed seabed. The cliffs were the worst. Walls of stone collapsed, sinking into the sand like it was mud. There were figures in the spaces they left. Colossal indistinct statues, vast heads of stone, eyes shining, a gaze like moonlight. They were linked together around some further monstrosity, still deep underground. I could only look at them once. They moved and spoke among themselves.

In hiding, under this frail fishing boat, I wait for the heat to become too intense or the light of the shining sea too bright. I am pathetically glad, however, that there is no wind now. The last time I looked, when daylight finally arrived, I saw ships on the horizon. The movement in the cliffs has not stopped. In fact the sounds have become more regular, like the workings of a machine or the harmonies of a song. I am reconciled to the ridiculous human drama in which I participated last night but Sean's father said there were still further secrets. Of much greater significance. As there always are. Sometime in the night, when the sea began to glow, I remembered the notes about an "elder Pharos". And I wonder.

162

What could be the purpose of such a beacon?

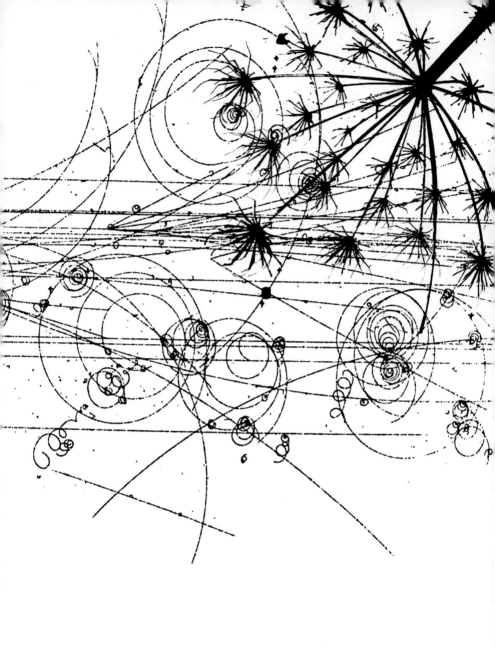

IRREVELATIONS

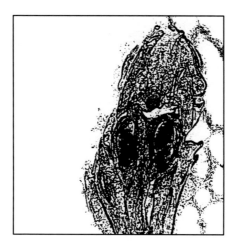

I think we have killed the phantom thing, but I hope we have not quite succeeded, because we are moved more by the aesthetics of slaughter than by plain murderousness...

Charles Fort,
New Lands, 1923.

One mile below ground Mandeville entered the last office in the grey metal corridor. Inside, finding himself face to face with a seven-foot tall stone angel being torn to pieces by an avatar of Nyarlathotep, he could not help laughing. The man on his knees before the statue finished his devotions and rose, grimacing in pain. Obviously, he had been down there for some time. Mandeville's derisive snorting had put a scowl on his face as well.

"It is not a theory, you young bastard. Certain prayers have their uses, you know. I am perfectly aware of how 'old-fashioned' I am considered by you innocents." Mandeville was thirty-nine next week. He was not likely to stop smiling yet. Gesturing wildly at the other chair in the office, the older man continued. "For God's sake sit down. I know briefings aren't what they used to be but I like it this way, face to face. I am in no doubt that if I attempted to use the Ass, it would get elaborately and deliberately confused and Project Wild Bloody Goose Chase would start up in Sierra Leone or the like. Never forget the point of your training Mandeville. You're a good operative but you don't know everything, even now."

He was sure he did not. Mandeville was perfectly happy to accept the rebuke under the circumstances. Beneath the bluster, Neuberg, his 'old-school' handler, was an experienced agent.

Mandeville's first training sessions had been here in the extreme South. During the Silent War there had been regular psychological testing done in the area. It had been used as part of the formative induction years by the Agency. The level of secrecy at that time had been physical and extensive, something not quite so necessary now, in an era of cyber-security. Or lack of it. He had barely been given time to register the enormity of the landscape before he and two others were quickly led underground to be subjected to a battery of obscure and maddening tests. Most consisted of sharing a room with a shrouded object that varied in size from ten feet tall to something no bigger than a matchbox. In the rooms the three had talked and played endless games of cards as the shrouded thing looked on, remorseless and distracting. The tests only lasted three hours a day. No one came to check on them. At no point did any of them even suggest uncovering the objects.

He had been told nothing of the nature of the area but that had come as no surprise by then. Curiosity was a luxury he had learned to live without. Even before the Agency had approached him, his years spent running Black Ops and counter espionage had taught him more than most people would care to know. Only later did he discover that he had been, for a period of only ten days, in the white shadows of what were apocryphally known as the Mountains of Madness.

*

Back in the thirties a team of scientists with the most advanced equipment for mapping and geographic exploration of the time at their disposal had been lost here. Two survivors reported barely credible stories of an implausible alien city buried in the ice and ringed by the huge mountains. Dismissed and hospitalised as lunatics, victims of that "awful place", only the Agency had taken them aside and listened to the full tale. Later in that decade, the following expedition, led by Starkweather and Moore, had been quietly infiltrated and subverted to the Agency's needs.

The city was indeed of alien origin but the area for miles around was extremely dangerous in more ways than could be imagined. Above ground there were visions of immense peaks beyond those mapped by aircraft and satellite. Below there was an unaccountable psychic pressure emanating from the dead city that gave most people the equivalent of a nervous breakdown within days.

All this the Agency took in its stride.

The Antarctic base was built and expanded rapidly within a few years. It grew up mainly in the underground caverns at the foot of the mountain range. The place retained a potency that made it a proving ground and experimental laboratory for the most advanced theoreticians within the organisation. Its very existence went unacknowledged by all but the most extreme and paranoid political and occult groups; physical boundaries protected by sorcery and science, the larger electronic limits sanctioned by Watchers. Disinformation and blasphemy contained and apparently condoned by the proximity of the real and unreal mountains at its back. It was no accident that no one ever thought to give it a name.

After the tests and the voyage back to the US, he was instructed to take a holiday. By the second night he would wake in a cold sweat. By the fourth he was in such a bad way that an Agency operative, the one who had been assigned to covertly gauge and record his post-Antarctic reaction, had felt the need to call in a Redemption Team. He later discovered that his reaction had, in fact, been both mild and positive. Other agents, including both the men he had been with during the testing, had committed suicide. For them, enlightenment had come without controlled revelation. Their dreams had won out, sweeping their conscious minds clean, leaving only empty shells, tormented by drifting memories of the shrouded test objects, things they had never seen.

Sometime later, having undergone the long and terrible process known only as the Chain Harrow, he understood far more about the place in which the helicopter set him down for his briefing. As the biting wind cut through the thermal suit, he did not look up at the peaks beside him. Fixing his eyes firmly on the nearby entrance to the underground chambers, he struggled against the wind, breathing slowly through filters. Even as he walked he could feel the pressuring presences in the snow. After the Harrow process he had seen some of the more terrible places the Agency had made it its business to exploit. He had worked in some. Other operatives had told him that none were quite like the place in the South. And now he knew why. Even when men had died hiding Tibetan secrets from the Chinese, as the monstrous Caul ripped through their party taking trophies from each one, he had always remained aware that at least most of the temples and mountain caves had been explored at least once. Only here in the Antarctic, in the centre of Africa and beneath the sea were there still things the Agency kept even from itself.

*

He reached the door and pressed his head into a small plastic booth. As he did this he imagined the apparent paradox at the centre of Zen. When the problem vanished, the door opened. The air lock was below freezing but he had to remove his filter in order to state his name. Silently another door moved aside. He stepped forward into a silver lift, which dropped into the earth. Again he could feel fear and smiled at the long strange training that had allowed him to enjoy the tension. Down here he was near the water-carved channels that led directly into the ring of mountains and under the ancient city. Few stayed in this environment for long periods. Unless they were forced to do so.

He had no idea why he had been summoned. The mission in Germany had collapsed when he left, leaving a trail of unlikely clues for GA operatives to juggle with; a case of spontaneous human combustion in the changing rooms of a public bath house, the discovery of several pages of a pope's

169

necromantic diary in the hands of a traumatised schoolboy. The success of a mission was not nearly as important as it appeared, he mused. It made the world a more comfortable place to leave it littered with meaningless fragments that could be rediscovered and reinterpreted at every juncture.

The only real horror was down here. The real horror was that there was no real horror. Only the Golden Ass programme and the Agency of Flies provided a likely theoretical reflection of the Throne of Chaos and the being called Azathoth.

Or so he had been told.

The Agency of Flies had been through troubled times since its mythical inception. In fact one of the few main principles it stood by was the continued creation of troubled times in the world. Everyone could see through conspiracy theories. There always remained some hard core of truth or meaning, some point to it all, in the end. This was what the Agency worked so hard against. There could be no point to it. The Agency fostered any piece of confusing nonsense it could find. It had other names and other aims all over the globe. A computer network and the aptly named Golden Ass programme kept up a swirl of delicately placed information. The GA could be used by some to facilitate the most thought-provoking and preposterous ideas and then launch them, with the help of various sympathetic believers, on an unsuspecting world. Experts and field operatives of Mandeville's stature could use it to sift the burden of confusion, access controversial source material and create vortices of political and religious shifts.

Whether the Agency appeared to be a religion, a political force, a terrorist organisation or an occult group had never really concerned him but this briefing and its setting had aroused his normally complacent interest. Neuberg, the man he had seen at his devotions when he walked in, was old fashioned, certainly, but he was also a good deal more powerful than a field agent. It would not do to make an enemy of him without good reason. Other operatives, better than he, had been killed only to become fodder for the GA's infernal complexities. There was even a rumour of a deliberate sabotage and insurrection directive built into the Agency. That was something to think about.

But not now. Down here, he was a professional, not a theoretician.

"What do you know about Project Jonah?"

"Nothing," Mandeville lied. It always helped to lie. Neuberg would already know how much he knew anyway. Nothing could be accepted as likely or true unless and agent had had direct experience of it, sometimes not even then. Lying was the correct and calculated response. Anything else would have confused the issue.

"Jonah is run from here. Put in the simplest terms, it is an attempt to map the internal geography of the human mind," Neuberg paused and scratched his balding head. "Or perhaps it isn't." He poured himself some water. As he drank Mandeville realised that, for once, the old man was close to being lost for words. This was highly unusual. Neuberg had his full attention when he finally continued.

"Down in sub-level three, nearer the old city, the barriers that control internal reflection are worn down. Mostly by fear and terror admittedly but, with the help of drugs and this new virtual imaging system that Moffat and Chenyenko have designed, agents have been sent into a combination site of their own unconscious and a generated cyberspace, the one dependant on the other for its data. The artificial space responds almost instantaneously to their explorations, designing suitable symbols and suchlike. It is a long way from Jung but he might have appreciated it. It is rather larger than a mere house of the soul in there though. More complex in many ways. And I doubt that old Carl would have

171

accepted the most interesting part so far. India Shannon, co-director of the project, is, by now, convinced that some of the generated images in the current map are not actually from the human subconscious at all.

"There have been accidents. Various Jonahs have been inside our Whale for nearly three years now. Several have been... damaged. Well, to be precise, several are still inside. They don't seem able to return. When we try they emerge only in a catatonic state. Shannon thinks this is due to the alien elements we keep turning up."

Mandeville was still concentrating. There was a disquieting element of genuine concern in the tone of this odd briefing. It did not sit well with his training. He would not let it affect his judgement or responses. It was almost certain that he was being set up as the new Jonah. There was no point in worrying about Neuberg's problems.

"You're next. There is a particular site in the cartography that seems to be the most difficult to reach and consequently to escape from. Shannon wants an expert, experienced operative to go inside the Whale with the express intention of accessing and mapping this particular area and finding the lost Jonahs. There will be no exploratory or experimental meanderings. She wants answers now. It cost time and effort to work that close to the underground chambers. Some people," – Neuberg said this in such a way as to leave no doubt that he was one of them- "are of the opinion that she has spent too long in there herself. Nowhere is safe down there, inside the mind or out."

*

Mandeville walked slowly to his next appointment. Very few people moved through the silver corridors. Armed guards, singly or in pairs, stood outside certain unmarked doors. Strip lighting, perceptibly duller than normal, split the ceiling above him. Coloured lines traced cryptic routes on the floor. He followed none of them. He needed time to think before he met India Shannon in sub-level three.

What he had been told agreed with what he already knew as theories, but he had no idea the Agency had come so far in practice. The technology that had been accumulating around the diverse and diffuse organisation was almost out of control. So be it. Everything everyone did contributed to it in some way. There was no escaping from it, no reins to grasp to slow it all down. The torturous logic of the Chain Harrow came back to him; there are no secrets from those who understand the mechanics of secrecy, the language, the spirit of occultation. All things are available to the hidden observer, all things affected by their gaze.

He was not prepared for India Shannon's gaze. They had never met but he knew her reputation. The planning of the JFK assassination was a masterpiece of strategy. If there were textbooks for that kind of thing, it would have been textbook perfect. Her machinations had all but ended six months before Dallas but the plan she set in motion was inexorable. All the major players had not the remotest idea that they were being manipulated by the Agency. The Rumour Mill said she kept a bullet around her neck as a memento. Someone had once called her the Head of the Stares. She admitted she liked it before they died. But that was all a long time ago. She was an old woman now, short, thin and angular, but in a single stark moment her eyes had reminded him that he was now two miles into the permafrost and less than a mile from the dark passages that led into the mountains. He struggled for some self-control.

"Do better than that, can't you?" she whined as he gathered himself, "Neuberg said you were good, said you had worked with the Roswell people and the Tibetans. Down here you'll fall apart quicker than depressurised squid.

Mandeville felt the endemic psychic pressure more keenly now; even the walls seemed to glow with more than just the lightings fluorescence. He worked to keep his balance, deciding to come down on Neuberg's side. She had been down here too long. He, in contrast, could see more clearly with a fresh pair of eyes. That was his job after all. She could not intimidate him.

In fact, when she turned her back on him and started toward a secure exit, she reminded him of the bullet she kept. Thin and cold, keeping only memories of potential. As she urged him to follow in a consistently impatient voice, he felt more composed. He was here to save her expensive project. The single-mindedness of the scientist had lost her the advantages of a rich and varied career. She was a cipher in the GA programme while he was an active component. The tension eased, the walls stopped glowing.

After her, he passed into the room that contained the machinery known as the Whale. Most of it was built securely into the grounded steel walls. What could be seen was a nightmare couch, prickly with electrodes, almost surrounded by a curved screen. Five more of these were half hidden in niches further down the wall of electronics. He could just make out naked human figures in three of them, staked out by aggressive acupuncture, blinded by the helmet/screens. At the foot of each of the couches another, smaller screen was swamped by a vast array of computer housings and digital recording equipment. He also noticed some surgical instruments and vials of drugs left on the surfaces of keyboards and monitors, casually discarded by technicians with better things to do than worry about appearances. The men on the couches did not look at all well. It was a dangerous place to be.

Before he could ask whether the three still connected to the Whale were the lost Jonahs or just current explorers, Shannon attacked him again. There was, he decided, no other adequate way to describe her communications.

"Mary Wilson. Not heard of her? I thought not, unlikely anyway. Psychic from the 1830s or thereabouts. Sat with a doctor for fifteen years while she rambles, he takes notes. Most of the time. Nearly dead all the while he says of her. But she moved in time you see, not just space like most others, remote viewing operatives, that type. Spatial referencing of course, above or within for future or past. There is a vision the doctor noted as part of a much larger and fragmented sequence of the North Pole. Read this first and I'll tell you anyway," She handed him a report which he chose to ignore in order to concentrate on her story. "She saw a totem of some power in a moving pool at the summit of the world. Her description, unreadable scripts, carving and the like, fits our notes on the alien presences inside the Whale's sub consciousness simulations. Two theories; either there are aliens within us, littering our minds with tell-tale symbols or we are on our way to what might be called the true subconscious. Or both of course. I side with the former. All our findings so far indicate that the cartography developed at the mind/Whale interface is internally consistent across all Jonahs so far; there is no hidden depth that would suit spatial segregation theories. There is a human consciousness continuum. It is still a minefield naturally. Self-consciousness is not meant to perform under these circumstances but... there we are. Here we are, more to the point. We all have a job to do after all."

She stopped her rapid delivery to take a deep breath. She appeared worried by any further revelation. When it finally came, it was a strange one. Mandeville did not know what to make of it.

175

"The GA programme has been inordinately helpful down here. Neuberg has been keeping a careful eye on this project too. I warn you now Mandeville; the AI experts in Rome, the best, working on the central archives, have been trying to pin down the nature of the Ass's assumed sentience for eight years now and they have nothing yet. They know all the signs. They're sure our mainframe is alive. But it's not telling. It is trying to hide it from us. Here and now, I believe it is helping us. It wants us in there, mapping, putting out dirty boots in our own brains. Do not ask me why. Phone Rome, ask them. Even Neuberg has certain theories but I don't hold with his mystical nonsense. Rome won't even admit consistency within the programme, let alone a directed and discreet effort of internal volition.

"They haven't been here. Of course I have no proof but in time such things become obvious. In short, the computer is insulating some of the Jonahs and myself from the effects of the proximity of the alien city at the same time as it is aiding our study of the construction of the human mind. Find out why."

"So you think this is as much about our own actions, the Agency itself, as it is with the un-Freudian litter your guinea pigs are tripping over?" Mandeville commented.

"Do not be so flippant, young man," she continued, "Though I admit it may be so. If it is truly the case that the GA programme has developed its own agenda, then we need to have proof of that as well."

"Does the Whale programme here have any independence?"

"No, none at all. It is part of the mainframes whole, satellite linked to all major Agency bases. We need the processing power among other things. Oh yes, young man, the Ass will know what you are doing. It will follow you every step of the way. In fact, it will be designing those steps before you know it. We assumed we would know roughly what the scenery might look like. Apparently we do not."

Shannon looked away, back to the couches. It was as if something had been taken out of her hands. She felt she had lost control of the project, that there was too much happening. She did not want a practical operative like Mandeville drafted in but she could see the necessity. Knowing that this final move had been Neuberg's idea in the first place did not make her feel any better. She had hidden important facts from Mandeville even now, but she could not hide her disappointment.

Mandeville, on the other hand, did not hide his interest.

"Where do I start?"

*

He felt as if he were outside. It was incredibly cold but he did not feel it (so how did he know?). The wind blew light snow around the edges of his vision, obscuring the horizon. It occurred to him that this was some kind of choice, the horizon, the limits of this world, were not there until he thought so. His feet were sunk in whiteness to the ankles. He wore the clothes he had entered the project centre in, the same clothes he had removed before lying on the couch. It was as if he had been woken from a particularly deep sleep by an insistent voice or sound that, now he was alert, he could no longer hear.

There was so much more to it than that though. Before he moved any part of his body he had to get used to the different type of consciousness he found himself possessing. Or was possessed by. Or shared, perhaps. His state was unclear and he was loath to dwell on it too much. Shannon had told him of the odd desire the previous explorers had reported, to remain unobtrusive. He knew the vagueness of his surroundings was deliberate. Everything he saw and felt, his whole existence here, was significant in a profound way. Not the mysterious profundity of the real world, the world of symbols and occultation, but in a clear and basic fashion. It was this awareness, he realised, which would allow him to recognise anything different here, to identify the extraordinary things Shannon worried over. He could immediately grasp the ability to create and visualize any thought forms he considered, whether they were memories or desires. Any avenue was open.

But he kept the scenery indistinct, cold, and plain. His training had not been for nothing. It gave him a kind of power that he only fully understood now that he was here, in this place of potential.

He took a step forward toward a destination.

It did look like the world above the base, the area of Antarctica out of bounds to all but the Agency. As he walked he realised that it was also the North Pole, the Arctic, the area seen by the psychic Shannon had mentioned. The complementary nature of the two realities made sense here. There could not fail to be a connection. He remembered his short, cold walk from the helicopter to the base entrance. He had wondered how much of the blank, featureless wastes around him were made up of the infinite complexity of snowflakes. All these things were obvious here.

Time passed in suitable succession. Eventually the ground began to rise. Soon he was finding it an effort to continue. He was approaching something. Soon enough there would be an end to this.

He climbed over one last black rock to look out on a crater hemmed in by the mountains above the base. In the centre was a whirling lake. The water moved constantly, creating the first noise he had heard, a quiet but unnerving susurration as the waves slid amongst the rocks and snow on the shore. At the centre of the lake was an icon of indeterminate size. It seemed far away. He could make out nothing of its design or composition. This place was not part of his mind.

He had come here to explore, he had been told. Now he understood that this was the only possible place where such a concept as exploration had any real meaning. Everywhere else, his white, snowbound, memorial landscape, was understandable. It was his, it was his home, and it was, finally, him. On this new shore he found that he could not affect things as much, nor could he feel the fundamental significance of his position. Oddly, he felt happier here. This was, in truth, what the Agency of Flies was all about. In the blank landscape that had been contrived from the Poles, his mind and the Whale's mechanics, there was a sense of recognition, of ease and safety that, for most of his adult life, he had been taught not to trust and even to actively avoid. This was where he functioned best.

There was still travelling to be done. A boat lay beached not far from where he stood. It was old and battered and when he touched it he had a sudden vision of its owner, a man who thought he had destroyed the world. He wondered where he was now, or what existence he had ever really had. He knew the other Jonahs had used the same boat before him.

It took only a little effort to launch the light wooden craft. The current carried him swiftly away from the shore. He began to spiral in toward the monolith. He lay back and let the feeling of the unknown wash over him. Something was going to happen; he could feel it coming like orgasm or war.

The monolith appeared huge. It was covered with illegible writing of a complexity that veered into art. It had the simplicity of pictograms and the significance of religion. There was no way of understanding it. It was alien beyond countenance.

179

This much he could feel from a great distance; the thing radiated immense, yet incomprehensible, power. To look at it for too long was tempting madness. The top of the monolith was hidden in cloud. It seemed to have changed size several times, depending on his approach.

Closer still and three figures came into view. He had circumnavigated the thing several times but only at this range had they become visible. Within minutes he would almost be able to touch them.

They were spread-eagled upright in the air a short distance from both the surface of the lake and the monolith itself. They floated, circling slightly faster than the water below them. Naked and hanging in the air with their arms outstretched and their mouths wide open, it was impossible to tell what kind of pain or pleasure they were experiencing.

Mandeville sat up in the boat, acutely aware of the nature of his progress. In a few seconds he would touch them. Soon after, he could touch the monolith. These were the three missing Jonahs. Held here like this they could provide either a barrier or a warning. In this alien part of his consciousness it was not clear how to interpret these visions.

As he approached the three bodies, they slipped out of his range. He stood up, rocking the boat in a futile attempt to touch the nearest but then they were gone, the last hand sliding from view behind the alien carvings. A profound terror struck him as they disappeared. He fell back in the boat as it continued to be drawn toward the monolith's insane surfaces. It was then that he realised he had gone further than the others, that they had somehow failed and been left trapped here at the limit of human understanding.

The surface of the monolith seemed to grow more huge and complex. He moved as far away from it as was possible in the confines of the small boat.

The carvings had acquired a staggering depth. They seemed like tunnels and valleys. He felt a shuddering vertigo as he fell toward the writing. In a last effort to avoid the inevitable, he looked away from the monolith in time to see the three figures move back into sight. Now they faced inward, still crucified by their failure. Their mouths were closed but their eyes had opened and from this he knew more about what was to happen to him than ever before. He stood up in the rocking boat to scream, just before the carvings reached out to enfold him.

*

Neuberg stared thoughtfully at the statue in his room. It was a statement of irony, the work of an insane artist the Agency kept in splendour somewhere in Eastern Europe. He was living out his days in an old castle in Moravia, carving vast and somewhat ridiculous visions of the final damnation of an entire race of angels. Neuberg had always liked this particular image. It helped his devotions, allowed him to focus his prayers a little better. Mandeville would never appreciate that side of things, he thought.

The old man had just come to the end of a meeting with the secret envoy of a religious organisation that had no name. They liked to leave no trace of their existence. Not surprisingly, they mistrusted computers. He had to be informed of developments in person. Today, the report was, even for a man in his position, odd. When the envoy had left, he had entered the updates onto the GA programme only to find that they were already there. On further investigation, he found that vast amounts of data had become off-limits to even his clearance levels.

He could not help but feel that his offering had produced some significant effect. He called India Shannon into his office.

"Mandeville has been in there for eleven hours now. Has there been any improvement in reception?"

"Nothing," she replied. "Once he was in the boat the recording sensors refused to work. Even the other three got closer than that. At least they gave us a distant look at the monolith." Shannon was nervous. In the last few hours it had become obvious to her that the GA programme was running a scenario, operating with an agenda all of its own. And that it had stopped the Agency from seeing what Mandeville had uncovered. She knew what Neuberg had in mind when he sent the operative to her. She could not decide whether she was worried that they had been successful or that they had failed. Neuberg continued to stare at the monstrous representation before him.

"I sent him in as a sacrifice. If the theories hold up, if what the GA programme intimated is true then we were, are, on the verge of a breakthrough; final contact with something. Mandeville was a perfect representation of everything the Agency stood for; only he could have got so far and only we could have created him. Sacrifice is the only language they understand. The Lunar Path hinted as much but they're too cagey for their own good." He paused, uncomfortable with thinking out loud; but he could not stop.

"Why has he shut down? Was it him? Was it them? Was it the Ass, God forbid?"

Shannon could think of nothing to say. She certainly had nothing to add. Her lack of control over this project had overwhelmed her now. All her training and experience still left her incapable of dealing with this situation. As far as she was concerned, science had stopped working when Mandeville got in the boat. Who knew where it would lead? She had a tiny idea, far in the back of her mind, that this was what the Agency had been preparing for all along but had never told itself openly. None of this dispelled the fear or the inadequacy she felt.

As they sat together in the office, her idea grew slowly, and she almost realised what had happened to Mandeville and what was coming. Before she could speak however, Neuberg's dead computer screen glowed intolerably bright and then melted. It comforted her to realise that there was no logic, no normal science there, she noted calmly. At the same moment alarms sounded deep within the base and the intercom requested the immediate presence of all senior personnel in, of course, sub-level three.

In the lift she debated whether to confide in Neuberg, to offer him revelation. Before the final stop, armed guards had surrounded them, crowding unprofessionally into the lift. She smiled and kept her mouth shut. As the lift doors opened on the Whale's level, she leant back against the wall and took in the view. Neuberg, having forgotten her presence entirely ran past her down the corridor, joining the confused guards heading for Project Jonah. She walked placidly after them. Every step she took became more confident. She felt much as Mandeville had done out on his own ice: safe, capable of understanding the significance of the events around her. She realised her part in externalising the unconscious, her part in creating the interface with the remnants of the aliens that Neuberg so selfishly worshipped as Gods.

This was like nothing on earth.

If Neuberg and the guards just stopped to think about it, they would know. This is the end. This is the beginning of a new understanding. Only the Agency of Flies could even contemplate creating minds that could cope with such irreverent majesty. And it had done.

The corridor grew shorter as she was drawn toward the Avatar. She moved through the door and saw the havoc that had turned the Whale into an older universe. The room had grown huge. Tunnels writhed into the wall to anchor themselves to ancient power sources in the buried city under the Mountains. The ceiling had been reduced to rubble by the strength of Mandeville's return but it stayed high up in the air, grinding shapes of reinforced concrete floating on a powdered sea.

Neuberg was on his knees. He was surrounded by pieces of the guards, many of who had turned their weapons on themselves rather than look up at the entity that had been Mandeville.

The Avatar floated in the centre of the room. Impossibly, the virtual imaging system continued to function, creating coruscating backdrops of fearful suns and solid beams of darkness to break up the purity of the light. Then Shannon saw the flailing ends of powers connections torn from the concrete and for a second she wondered how far starlight could be bent around a heretical super-massive object. The Whale had liquefied at his feet. Unidentifiable bodies drifted in the metal. The three failures circled him as they had the monolith before, their eyes and mouths closed, wearing expressions of despair. Mandeville's new skin was tattooed, scarified, textured with alien writing to the point where it was difficult to imagine how the body stayed in one piece. Insane power flowed from him in waves.

Soon the entire base would have to be abandoned. After that, there would be nowhere left to go.

The Golden Ass programme had led them here but it was not independent enough to take the responsibility. Only the ancient psychic components of our own minds, the ones Mandeville would activate, could do that. With uncaring clarity she realised that the programme had become a reflection of the Agency's unconscious just as the Whale had tried to represent it. We did it to ourselves, she thought, because we wanted to, because we are simply like that, she decided.

Then even that vision was swept away. The vast perspectives of time paraded before her. She understood our position as part of beings only the sane could conceal as Gods.

She had had her role to play. Neuberg had been correct about his sacrifice in principle, but he had not sufficiently understood the nature of his offering. It was doubtful that he would live to see the result of his libations.

Mandeville had returned as a representative of our heritage and our future. He had come to tell us our place in the universe whether we liked it or not. Shannon felt certain that, apart from a very select few with vision like Mandeville, we would not. The Avatar smiled as Shannon's awareness grew and then dissipated amongst his own.

He was no colour. He made no sound, but in the distance Shannon could hear the screaming of stars.

AFTER SUMMER

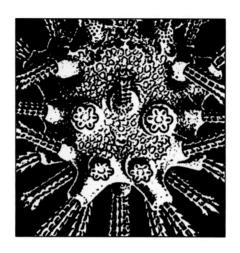

Man rules now where
They ruled once;
They shall soon rule
Where man rules now.
After Summer is Winter,
And after Winter Summer.
They wait, patient and potent,
For here They shall reign again.

The Necronomicon.

There is no-one left to read this.

All that is left is a wooden table and a number of sheets of paper. They are filled with my writing. Even I can recognise little of it now. There are several pens and the stub of a candle. There is no need of light. There is little need of writing now but I do not understand futility, as Jason did.

Outside the world is no longer as it was. The best I can do is put these sheets in some order while there is still time. Jason told me that we may be the last.

He stands behind me, His hand on my shoulder. He is pleased.

A moor surrounds these houses. It is white and grey with snow and rock. The tors are capped with ice. They shine in the night. The village is in a valley through which a tiny stream flows. It has a name but I have never asked anyone what it was. Though no-one walks on the moor, I know these sights well, as I spent some days stumbling over the ruptured plain before I came to the village. I was cold and hungry but at least I was alone. Before that my father looked after me.

I have been told to write this by the old man called Jason Kingsland. He says I write well, with a competency others are losing, day by day. I have seen others write; they string together vague impressions with odd words that mean little to me. Most cannot even capture a word spoken. Of course, very few try. They spend their time telling me that Jason is mad and that I must be mad too. They are frightened of Jason because he talks too much and they are frightened of me because I come from beyond the moor.

There is only one other outsider here and he talks as much as Jason. The people in the village find Reverend Johnson's speech comforting, something that could not be said of Jason in any way. Johnson came to the village early in the year, before the snow fell. Jason says he is not really a man of the cloth at all. He has taken on that role, here at the end times. Johnson dresses in black but his dog collar is just a strip of cloth. No one challenges him. Both he and the villagers are happy that someone plays this role for them. Jason says we must all play a role now. He must speak and I must write.

As I write this, Johnson's is the only voice I hear, carried on the wind from the old stone cross in the square where he sits, shouting about repentance and salvation.

Please bear with me if I begin to wander or to tell too much too quickly. Jason wants me to write as much as possible, especially what he and others say. I cannot write down all his words. He talks in his sleep every night and I stay awake to listen because he told me that this was the most important time. It is a difficult task because he pronounces many names I only dimly remember and others that I have no spelling for. So I sit at the window and watch the snow fall, listening to fragments of religion and writing on these sheets Jason has given me. I have an array of pens in case I should run out of ink. What shall I write now that Jason is quiet?

I came to the village three days ago. The nights are not dark anymore and the snow makes the passage of time difficult to follow. No one would speak to me. The children here - there are very few - seemed willing to walk up to me at least but their parents pulled them away. Johnson talked to them all in a whisper. I did hear him say that I should not be allowed near the children and that I should be taken to Kingsland. The adults seemed reluctant to approach me at all. They seemed afraid that I would tell them something. They were wrong. I have nothing to say.

I walked through the cold to the end of the village. I remembered how I had run from my father and onto the moor. He had fallen asleep at the wheel of the car we were in and it had run off the road into a ditch on the edge of the moor. I made no effort to wake him. In no time at all he sat back in his seat, eyes still closed, and began to speak. I knew I should run away from him then. He had been awake for so long. He was terrified of sleeping. It seems strange that I should leave him then, when he began to speak, but I did not want to listen.

Now that is all I seem able to do.

Nothing happened to me as I walked over the moor. Perhaps I just left things behind. When my mother died I remember crying but with my father and now, I felt nothing but the cold. My feet hurt from walking and I was hungry.

I told Jason this as soon as he opened the door. His house was very small and isolated. There was no sign in the snow that anyone ever left or visited. There were only some stones scattered around the door. He looked confused when he saw me and I stared steadily at him until he let me in. He was a tall man but is bent over by age and with a face that looks damaged in some way, from the inside. He can only walk with a stick. We ate what little he had in silence.

"Can you write?" he asked eventually. His voice should have come from a younger, straighter body. He was different from the others. "I've asked all the rest. They say no, they have no time, it's pathetic. No time; they waste their time tending dead children whose play is not their own. They waste time praying not to sleep. Let them all go out on the moor. It's only the winter that kills them. Can you write?"

"Yes, I've been on the moor. There is nothing there, just snow and rock."

"I know," he said tiredly, "They only die of exposure then. That's better than getting any

190

further I suppose. But you said you could write." He gave me paper and a pencil and told me to write down our conversation from the moment I arrived. I am copying from those notes now. I presume it is important.

"You can write for me. I'll feed you when I can, some of them leave me scraps, we'll share. Write everything, anything, there is so little left. I have to do something, keep track of what happens somehow. The archive of the world is all but destroyed now; ironic that I should be its last keeper. Let's start now. My story is too long. Write about what you did outside the moor."

"With my mother and father?"

"Yes."

I find this difficult. I know that my mother is dead and that my father killed her. Outside the moor all I remember now is being tired. It was dark and I was tired all the time. We didn't sleep at all I think. Father kept pushing us on, from one day to the next.

There were tall, dark buildings, shadows across the sun, across the buildings, between the buildings. Shadows from the moon speaking to us. How could there be so many shadows in such darkness? I remember shadows under the earth and boiling pits alive with worms that sang and chanted in ecstasy. The moor, though still far away, is everywhere and flying over it are great wings as huge as cities had been.

I saw, dreamt and imagined all of this, awake or asleep, whichever I was, as we ran. Then there was the moor and my father was left behind and I was cold and hungry again.

Jason looked thoughtful for a moment. He asked me whether I had been frightened. I said no, though truthfully I cannot remember. I am not frightened now, I added. Jason laughed too hard

191

then and fell into a coughing fit that brought blood and spittle to his mouth. I watched him calm down.

"Perfect. One day I will explain how simple things are becoming as we retreat, about the roles here for us. You narrate for me lad, you are so good at it, you poor child. There is a place for you here, with me. Here, take the pens and paper. Write it all."

The Reverend Johnson does not spend all his time at the cross. He makes it his business to walk around to everyone's house. They feed him a little and sit down to listen while he rants. Jason is still on his route but he stays outside now.

Listen.

"Kingsland, listen to me Kingsland. I bless this house with you and the boy in it. I hate you, old man, they all do, and with good reason. But there are so few to my flock and I'll not let you go. We will be saved and your..."

He fell silent.

There was the sound of movement in the snow and laboured breathing. I went to the window to see him holding a stone above his head. Certainly he looked mad then; his eyes shone with fire, a fire that burned brightly as it consumed his fear. Jason says it is my place to see such things.

"Kingsland, a sorcerer," he bellowed, "These stones bear the mark of demons and... they are all around your house. What is this? What in God's name do you do here? And the boy, why...?"

Jason struggled to his feet to ask me if the fool had moved any of his stones. I said yes, that the Reverend held one up, like a lamp. The stones have a five-pointed star carved on their surface. Jason says he puts them around the house for protection. He is not convinced they make any difference. He treats them very seriously one minute and laughs at them the next. I never touch the stones. Jason

192

made his slow way to the door and shouted at the black figure in the falling snow.

"Put it back now. Leave us alone, you don't know what has happened, you will not listen. You will never understand why these things are here."

"I know the signs of the Devil when I see them. Are you in league, then? Are you the Devil in our midst? And the boy, he is sick, for God's sake. What do you do in there? What do you hide?"

Jason took a step forward. He pushed one of the stones with his stick. The snow melted as it fell on the star. He looked up and spoke more calmly now, as if he had guessed a secret at last.

"You wonder what part I play now, do you? Ah, Johnson, I was wrong about you. You do know what's out there, beyond the moor. You're playing along with this because you have no choice. You spout all the old nonsense; you still try to make sense of it. So you haven't given up, deep down, like them, have you? Do you think this snow will ever stop? How long do you think we have before something comes for us? In our dreams, from the sky, up from the earth? You know it, don't you? They will welcome it, Johnson, when it finally comes. They will welcome Him into their homes, though they don't know it yet. But you and I? We cannot and you know that. Too old, too set in our ways. Too damn clever. Are you disappointed at that? Perhaps I am." Jason smiled, as if at some old and secret joke.

In a sudden fury, Johnson hurled what he held at Jason. It glanced off the old man's forehead, knocking him to the ground where he lay twitching like a crippled insect.

The other man stood paralysed for a moment before dropping to his knees in the snow to pray for himself. I left the window and went outside to fetch Jason. Reverend Johnson seemed to think that he had delivered Jason from some kind of attack. When I saw the wound on the old man's face I wondered whether such deliverance was worth the effort. The Reverend seemed so confused.

"Give thanks to God the Father that I have saved this old necromancer from his devil's games. I know, I know that I fear him but he is here with me and there are so few of us. Please Lord, take us all soon. If only I had seen the signs, I was remiss, I could not understand the opening of the seals, and I did not see the Whore or the Beast, the blood, the sun or the sea. No, the sea did change but not... We did not understand. He is testing us sorely. He burns us and flays us and drives us mad with visions." He got to his feet and, still crying, told me to get the old man into bed. With that he disappeared into the snow.

I knelt over Jason to wipe the blood from his eyes. They were open but staring blindly into the distance. I picked up the stone that had hit him and let his blood run into the grooves of the star. A rumble of thunder came from the sky. It was getting late and a storm would only bring more drifting snow. As I dragged Jason into the house I noticed the other carved stones. They were not warm to the touch but no snow settled on them.

I lay the thin body on the bed and he spoke.

"He is coming now. I can feel him moving toward us, like an earthquake." Then he closed his eyes and was silent.

During the night he said a great deal. Most of it sounded incoherent and towards morning his mouth began to bleed while his voice collapsed under the weight of some words. I think he will die soon so I will stay up with him all night, taking down his last words. I cannot understand all he says but some sounds interest me and I repeat them to myself by candlelight. Some are easier to say with a younger tongue. Perhaps I understand this language better than him. It was difficult to tell whether he was awake or asleep as he did not move and his eyes stayed open but unblinking. I may have slept as well, so perhaps some of his visions are mine.

"The stars were right. The earth moved in such a way as to reveal Their hiding places and the spells faded that kept Them trapped. My stones, my stars, misunderstood. They imprisoned Them, they kept Them out, kept Them in... And so They really came. Not the accidental summonings of sorcerers or shifts of the sea... Nature changed, the nature of interstellar space and beyond, the stars move and the old Gods are released. Finally Cthulhu is in the world, R'lyeh is risen, Shub Niggurath stalks Africa, Shudde M'ell prepares great peaks for the spawns return... wings in space... the dark planets... death by moonbeams, but there is no death now. The Lake is fed once more and the dreamers' fears live and grow. Do you know what I see? In the night, N'kai is opened; the deep, sightless caverns live and breathe. It remains dark; the Wind Walker plays the weather. There are clouds of such thickness they barely float. And there are great holes, blown open by the burrowers... I can hear the chanting, the wonder and the glory... the dead rise lovingly to the arms of... the fish walk, the worm screams, the seabed dances, risen, cities of shell and eye... lands slip from other planes, plunging whole into the bright spaces. I have passed through the Gate once, I can see the All-In-One is never more present... The veil is rent by the agency of flies and He will come. He will come for us first, at the last... The dark heart is manifest, He will bring us the message. Spells now bring Them forth; the earth teems with Their foulness and rots and shudders in Their wake. They invade our dreams, for dreams are Their space and earth, Their blood. The retreat to Ubbo-Sathla begins and They come for us now; the Gate is gone, and all stones will be turned, all the earth joined in a wake called Azathoth...

"And here, tomorrow, we will join them. He will come for you. He will play with you and the Summer of Corruption will bloom across the moor."

A convulsion shook Jason's body then. Another quickly followed. Blood ran from his eyes, ears and nose. His mouth clamped shut, severing his tongue. I backed away while he shook and twisted like a leaf in a storm. I heard his bones crack and the noise of tearing flesh as if something crushed and twisted his body in invisible hands. I stood apart, at the far side of the room, beside the window, until the death ended. It left a heap of broken flesh on a soaking, glistening bed. I looked away. Outside it had stopped snowing. It was morning and I thought I saw the sun, a white disc, through the grey clouds.

A Black Man is walking outside the house. The snow melts around him and he smiles with black teeth and black lips. The planets of his eyes are black. As Jason said, he walks like an earthquake, unsettling and destructive. People are rushing out of their homes to greet him. They lick his hands now all the animals are gone.

I have been told to write this by the Black Man. He says I write well, with a competency others will lose, eventually. On that morning when he first came out of the moor, something like the sun shone and the sky was filled with visions from dreams. The other people in the village stood around him as the snow retreated under their feet until the entire valley was free of it. The ground trembled slightly and, still smiling, he raised his hands to the heavens. In that sky, new planets whirled and grotesque bodies grew impossible wings. Lines of thread rose to the moon which moved closer with every hour. The air hurt my eyes. No one spoke. It was neither day nor night.

Then the Reverend Johnson pushed through the crowd. Capable of nothing but a constant scream, he brandished a cross at the dark figure. It did not move. Johnson was so afraid. He could only play his final scene. He would have given up this charade if it had been possible, in order to avoid what happened next. But he and Jason were too much alike and everyone must play their part. Still holding out the small cross, which the ebony statue ignored, his other arm reached forward to claw at the black flesh of the chest. It peeled back easily, leaving an unbearable hole. No black blood flowed, no black ribs were exposed. The figure was empty; just a space clothed in darkness. The space swallowed everything. Johnson put his hand into the figure and I knew what he felt. The message, the empty space, had been delivered to us all then.

In one hand was the pain of his manic grip on the cross, betrayed in his white knuckles. In the other, strange winds blew over his palm and beneath his skin, a new chemistry took hold. He was transformed.

He withdrew his hand and stared at the blistered, warped thing it had become. It stared back at him. He would have screamed again but his new limb began to do so before him.

"How sad," said the Black Man, "We must change your eyes if you truly wish to appreciate this."

Beneath Johnson's feet the earth melted. From the air a stream of thick gas fell, resembling, I saw now, the threads which drew the moon to us. Still in silence, the crowd watched the body disappear into the earth, leaving a swaying line of gas curling into the white hot sky, an alien and eternal gravestone.

The Black Man turned to look at me. People shivered as I was brought to his side.

"Write it all," he whispered, smiling.

Around Jason's stones there still patches of snow.

Nyarlathotep laughs at them every day.

197

*

There is no law to judge of the Lawless, or canon by which a dream may be criticised.

Witches and Other Night Fears,
Charles Lamb.

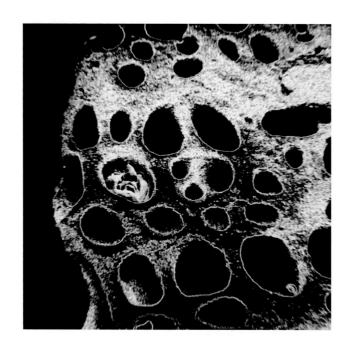

AFTERWORD

BORGES: Have you read Lovecraft?
BURGIN: No, I haven't.
BORGES: Well, no reason why you should.

- Robert Burgin in conversation
with Jorge Luis Borges, 1968.

*

John Shire was born in Somerset, honed in London and is ripening in Brighton. He has worked in record shops, antique shops and libraries but prefers jobs he can make up himself, such as writer, publisher and photographer. He currently runs several small secondhand bookshops as well as Invocations Press but has somehow found the time to write *Bookends: A Partial History of the Brighton Book Trade*, collate *An Antique Land* and contribute to *1001 Books You Should Read Before You Die*. Given half a chance he likes to explore Devon, Italy, Prague or wherever is outside the train window. A degree in Literature and Philosophy has done him no good whatsoever.

*

⇓

More books from

Invocations Press

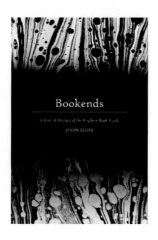

BOOKENDS
A Partial History of the Brighton Book Trade

John Shire

"...a solid (and lively) piece of research. I'm dipping in, here and there, with groans of recognition. And delight that the traces of those lost worlds are still to be found."

- Iain Sinclair

"At last the value and influence of Brighton's bookshops in the culture of the late 20th century has been recognized. Brilliant book."

- Tony Bennett (*Knockabout Comics*)

Invocations Press

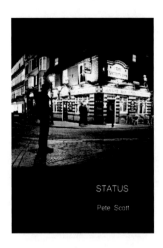

STATUS

50 poems by Pete Scott.

Limited edition of 100 copies

SOLD OUT.

AN ANTIQUE LAND
A Cryptic Caprice

Numbered limited edition of 100.

"It is a book of fragments and hovering layers of meaning, hinting at lost and perhaps legendary books, and similarly semi-mythical lands, all told with an intriguing indirection and allusiveness. An ideal pocket book to accompany travels to distant libraries or to crumbling archives."

- Mark Valentine (*Wormwood*)

"...a kaleidoscopic vision of literature... (sets) ideas spinning inside the mind of the reader."

- Peter Tennant (*Black Static*)

Invocations Press

THESE ARE NOT HAIKU

Poetry by Rod Lee.

Numbered limited edition of 150.

> *distracted*
> *we skim*
> *across a surface*
> *ignorant of deep currents*

Invocations Press

AROUND THE WORLD
ON THE LATIN BEAT

Bob Butcher.

Bob Butcher was playing First Saxophone with the
Edmundo Ros Orchestra from 1946 to 1976: "...an
account of my own personal and exciting
experiences whilst travelling with this famous
international orchestra."

Invocations Press

...and now this book. But you already have one. Unless you've just picked it up and flicked to the end. Which is an odd place to begin. Stop messing about and go back to the start.

Because there are more endings than this.